MATED UNDER THE MISTLETOE

A VALE VALLEY WINTER ROMANCE

CONNOR CROWE

FATED FIRE FOUNDRY

One last summer. One last chance.

Sign up here for a FREE Love in Diamond Falls prequel - *Summer Heat*

https://dl.bookfunnel.com/ntkicsmnr6

Join my Facebook group Connor's Coven for live streams, giveaways, and sneak peeks. It's the most fun you can have without being arrested ;)

https://www.facebook.com/groups/connorscoven/

THE PHONE CALL

SEBASTIAN

"Merry Christmas, Mr. Wallace!"

Hannah poked her head into my office, brandishing a glittery card and a very festive looking cupcake.

A quick glance at the calendar on my desktop read December 1. I turned to Hannah and gave her my best smile. "You going to keep doing this every day till Christmas?" I asked. "There's still a whole month left."

She gave me her best pouty face. "And who says I can't start celebrating early? Besides, if there's cupcakes in it for you, you can't be too grumpy about it."

She had a point. I shrugged and took the card and cupcake from her, setting them on my desk next to all the day's paperwork. "Thank you, Hannah." I turned back to her. "And you know you can call me Sebastian. I may be the CEO, but I don't want anyone to feel they can't approach me. We're in this together."

Hannah bobbed her head up and down. The tight black ponytail she always wore bounced from side to side, and that's when I realized: she was wearing a jingle bells hair tie.

Lord, this was gonna be a long month.

"Of course, Mr.—I mean Sebastian. Can I call you Seb? I was coming in here to let you know I'm traveling for the holidays starting December 12th. My family has this whole crazy 12 days of Christmas tradition, and I couldn't miss it..."

The twelfth. So soon.

I rubbed my forehead, trying to come up with a response. But she looked so excited about going home, so sure that I'd say yes, that I couldn't resist.

"Oh, all right. But you know we have some big deadlines coming up. Think you'll be able to finish your work before you leave?"

"I will, promise. Thank you Seb!" With that, she bounced out the door, her musical hair tie ringing as she went.

The door clattered closed and I returned to the computer. Less than a month until Christmas. And so much yet to do.

I wondered why I'd given in so easily to Hannah's request. I wasn't exactly known for being the most festive this time of year. But there was a reason for that.

When I saw Hannah's eyes light up as she talked about her family, it touched something inside me. Something I'd lost, long ago. Hope? Happiness? Joy for the future?

Didn't matter now though. What mattered was closing this deal before Christmas. Everyone knew nearly the entire month of December was a dead zone for work getting done, but it wasn't like I had a choice.

I'd busted my ass getting Wallace Innovations off the ground, and now we were one of the up and coming consulting firms in New York City.

That came with a price, though. My people were feeling the strain of all the work, and I was too, much as I didn't want to admit it. Our reputation for quick and stellar service meant we were working basically all the time, and while it was fun at first, lost in the heady haze of adrenaline and bootstrapping the business, it was starting to wear on us. All of us.

I ran a hand through my hair and stared at the

computer screen, my eyes glazing over. Deep inside, my dragon roared. It didn't like being cooped up like this. I knew that much. But I'd never asked to be a shifter. Especially in the cutthroat world of business, coming out as a shifter would only be a liability. So I kept to myself and buried those parts of me deep, deep within.

I left my hometown as soon as I could and set off for the big city. I didn't want any part of their games. I wanted to prove to myself that I could be more than nature had decided for me.

And it worked. Sorta.

With an MBA in hand, they said I'd have my pick of opportunities. So what did I do? Started my own business, of course. Something about me and authority never really meshed too well. Hell, I nearly got kicked out of school a couple times. But I remembered why I was there in the first place and doubled down. Tripled down.

I needed school, just as I needed to keep my shifter at bay. I needed routine and discipline to make up for my weaknesses. And there were many.

When's the last time you've stretched your wings? A little voice came from within. I shook my head and squinted at the spreadsheet even more aggressively, like that would make the thoughts go away.

You need to get out. A dragon isn't meant to be cooped up in an office.

"I'm not a dragon," I muttered through gritted teeth. "I'm a man."

And an alpha, it teased. *When are you going to find a mate?*

When I'm done here, was the first answer that came to mind, but it wasn't a good one. Anyone could tell you that any endeavor, creative or otherwise, was never truly done. You simply built it the best you could and then took that leap of faith, putting it out into the world.

Yeah. It was that leaping part I wasn't so good at sometimes.

My thoughts returned to Hannah's jingling pigtails and the festive cheer on her face when mentioning going home for Christmas. Had I stayed in Vale Valley, there probably would have been a huge celebration for the season. There always was, at least when I was a kid. All the shifters got together and ran, flew, or swam free, the night of Christmas Eve. A way to ring in the season.

But my favorite part of it all? No question. The yearly

Festival of Fire was one of the things I missed most about Vale Valley. That and Rosemary Vale. She was the mayor of the town and one of the sweetest old ladies I'd ever met. I almost regretted leaving her when I 'spread my wings' after high school and left town. Always there with a kind word or a helping hand, she seemed to be everywhere at once, and had an uncanny knack for knowing what others wanted or needed, even when they didn't quite know it themselves.

Growing up in Vale Valley, it wasn't that weird, though. It was an enclave of shifters and non shifters alike, held in balance by a magical force field around the town. A spell hung over the valley, ensuring that only the full hearted would ever find the place.

If you're lost and need love and a warm home, Vale Valley will be there for you.

I mouthed the words of our hometown slogan. So cheery. So cheesy. So...optimistic. They lived in a bubble, without a care for the goings-on of the real world. More than a little irresponsible, if you asked me.

But they'd made their choices. Just as I'd made mine. And business was picking up here in NYC. Just had to dig myself and my team out from under this mountain of work we'd created for ourselves...

The phone rang and I startled, jostling the cup of pens on the desk and sending them flying.

I cleared my throat and grabbed the phone, taking a quick moment to exhale and ground myself.

"Hello, Wallace Innovations. This is Sebastian Wallace speaking."

"Sebastian. Oh, thank god I got the right number. I wasn't sure, took me quite a bit of digging to find you out there in the wide world."

I froze. I knew that voice. Hadn't heard it in years, but still I knew it like the back of my hand.

That was Rosemary Vale.

"Rose," I breathed. "How'd you find me?"

"You know I've always had a knack for that, sweetheart."

I huffed in amusement. "I know. But why now?"

She grew silent for a moment, then choose her words carefully. "I wish I was contacting you under better circumstances, Sebastian. But it's your mother."

I froze. Blinked. Surely I hadn't heard that right.

"Sebastian?" Rose asked on the other line. "You there?"

"Yeah," I croaked. "What happened to her?"

When I left Vale Valley, I hadn't done so on the best of terms. I was ready to get out and see the world. I was ready to take life into my own hands, something I hadn't quite been able to do back at home.

Silence strung out on the end of the line. A lump built up in my throat. Sure, I left out of rebellion and anger, but if something had happened to her...

"I hate to be the one to tell you this, Seb. But Nellie died in her sleep last night. Totally unexpected, mind you. But she went peacefully."

I gripped the phone so hard my knuckles hurt. "Wha-?" I stammered. She didn't actually say 'died'. She didn't.

"I'm so sorry, Sebastian. Your mother has passed away."

Memories flooded back all at once. I drowned in them. All the things I'd never told her. And all the things I wish I could have done, could have said...

She went to her grave believing that her only son had abandoned her.

I vaguely heard Rose's voice on the other end of the line, but she sounded far away now. Distant.

"It was sudden, but she had a rough will drafted up not long ago. She was in perfect health beforehand, far as we could tell. But these things happen sometimes, unfortunately. The only problem now is her estate. Since you're the next-of-kin, you need to be here."

"I...yeah. When?" My mind spun. There was so much left to finish here, but if my mom was dead, did it even matter?

"Vale Valley needs you, Sebastian." Rose echoed the same words that had been on my mind. "It's time to come home."

"Yeah," I breathed, scrabbling around on the desk for something to write with. "I'll get there on the next flight out. I...let me just notify my staff."

"See you soon, Sebastian. You know Vale Valley will always be here to welcome you home."

I sat there for a few moments in the silence of the office. How things had changed. Nothing like a death in the family to get you to re-evaluate your priorities.

Even if we weren't ever very close...in fact, because of that, it felt so much more raw. Like the rug had been ripped out from under me with no warning, no chance to make things right.

I'd never get the chance to make amends with her. Never again get the chance to tell her I loved her. It wasn't fair.

No, more than that. It was wrong. This wasn't supposed to happen!

My dragon reared up inside me, screeching in pain and grief. *Gone!* It shrieked. *She's gone! Mother!*

Everything felt cold. Distant. Out of touch. There was a knock at my door, but I barely even registered it.

I needed to tell the team. Then I needed to get my ass to Vale Valley.

GHOSTS AND GARLANDS

WILL

"Thank you, have a nice day!" I called to the last customer as he left with two huge pots of poinsettias.

Whew. Another long day at Vale Valley's premier garden and landscaping shop. I brushed my dirty hands on my apron and went to check on the plants. We didn't sell trees here, no, but for just about every other kind of festive plant or decoration, people came to us.

I'd been on my feet all day, and even though I'd slept more than usual the night before, I felt like I was about to fall asleep. Mentally running through the closing-up-shop list in my mind, I was already picturing a hot shower and a cozy blanket.

At least, that was what I wished I could be doing. As it stood, I had a little problem.

A ghostly form poked its head through the glass, peering right at me. I flinched back a few steps. I managed not to scream this time, but my heart still raced.

"It's you again," the voice said in a wispy, ethereal voice. It floated through the walls and glass as easily as if they were smoke. Lifeless eyes followed me. "We're not supposed to be able to see you."

I huffed. "I'm not supposed to be able to see you, is more like it. Get out of the way, so I can lock up and go home."

Not again.

For whatever reason, I had the ability to see ghosts. Spirits. Dead people, if you wanted to call them that. And dead people, as it turns out, are extraordinarily chatty. Not to mention they always pop up at exactly the wrong time, like that annoying neighbor you can never seem to avoid.

"It's Nellie, Will," the ghost said. "Over at the Dozing Dragon."

I cocked an eyebrow. I'd been over there more than a few times. After all, Nellie was one of my best customers. Since she and her family were dragon shifters, they'd named the place The Dozing Dragon as a cute play on words. She loved color. Loved flowers. We made deliveries over there just about weekly, with the most outrageous stuff I could find and put together.

But what did that have to do with anything? Come to think of it, I hadn't seen her in the shop in quite a while...

I was pushing through the door, trying to ignore the nagging voices altogether, when the spirit spoke next.

"The Dozing Dragon is closed. Saw the sign just today. You will too if you go up the hill and look."

My hand froze on the doorknob. Closed. That couldn't be possible. This was peak travel time for Vale Valley. The Bed and Breakfast was always booked months out in advance this time of year, and the Christmas dinners Nellie cooked up were nothing short of legendary.

"What are you talking about, closed?" I asked when I found my voice.

"We felt her pass over," the spirit wailed in a mournful sigh. "To our side. She's...she's dead."

"What?" I cried. "Is this your idea of a joke? Really tired

of you guys popping up everywhere when I'm just trying to live my life. Go haunt someone else."

The spirit sighed, if spirits could sigh. A rush of cold air hit my back, and I shivered.

"Leave me alone," I said through gritted teeth.

"Wish we could," the spirit wailed, floating along beside me when I barged out the doors and bent down to lock up. "But something's keeping us around. We can't move on from here any more than you can."

I tried to make sense of their words. Vale Valley was no stranger to supernatural occurrences, sure, but speaking to the dead? Trapped spirits that only I could see? That was just crazy.

Maybe I'd been working too hard. Maybe I needed some sleep. Or a strong drink. Or both.

I walked down the path home, shoving my hands in my pockets for warmth. My boots crunched in the packed snow and I wrapped my scarf tighter around my neck. The icy wind picked up as the sun went down, making the air even chillier than usual. As much as I loved Christmas and all the holiday cheer that went along with it, I could do without the cold, thank you very much. I was small, even for an omega, and I didn't really retain heat that well. No insulation, I joked.

So I gathered the puffy coat around my waist and hurried on home, trying to ignore the wispy spirit trailing behind me.

"If she's really dead," I said without looking behind me. I knew he was still there. He didn't have anywhere else to go. Nothing else to do but to harass me, apparently. "Then why haven't I heard anything about it yet? News travels fast here in the valley. It would be all over town by now."

"Or maybe you were too caught up with all the holiday orders to open your eyes and ears. Maybe, Will, you don't want to see what's happening around you."

I frowned. My hands clenched into fists in my coat pockets and I clenched my jaw together. That wasn't true. I paid plenty attention. Some might say too much attention, since apparently I was the only person seeing these spirits. I didn't want to deal with them and their problems. I had enough going on in my own life.

And at the root of it all, I was scared. Who could I even tell about this? We had witches, shifters, supernaturals of all kinds, but those...well, made sense. This? Having dead people following me around? Not exactly common.

And, well, I'd tried so hard to fit in here. Not to make

waves. I wanted a 'normal' life. Normal as one gets in Vale Valley, anyway. I respected all the supernaturals around us, and it had given me a very diverse outlook on life and the world, but me? No. I was simply Will. Never did too well at school. Never was told I was going to 'amount' to anything. Not to mention, growing up being able to see the spirits of the dead kinda put a damper on my social life. Plants were about the only thing that calmed me. The only things that didn't judge me during those tough transitionary years between childhood and adulthood. I'd always been a little too nerdy. A little too awkward. A little too...omega.

So I kept my head down. Did what I did best. Moved to Vale Valley, opened a plant nursery, and took each moment as it came.

Today, I was tired. Tired of being on my feet. Tired of filling way too many orders in way too little time. I wanted to go home and cook dinner and rest. Not deal with naggy ghosts. It didn't look like I was gonna get that luxury.

By the time I made it home, my ghostly pursuer had disappeared. They always did, eventually. I didn't know where they went, but as long as they weren't bothering me? Not my problem.

I dropped my keys into the bowl by the door and

checked the crockpot in the kitchen. As soon as I stepped in the door the scent of beef and veggies hit me. Crockpots were probably one of the best inventions ever, in my opinion. I could toss in all the ingredients in the morning, turn it on, and have a piping hot meal ready when I got home from the nursery.

Even as I sat down for my dinner, though, I couldn't help but think about what the spirit had told me. Nellie, the well-loved owner of The Dozing Dragon B&B, had died. Could it really be true?

Nellie was almost as much of a staple of this little old town as Rosemary Vale herself. Nellie Wallace seemed to know everyone by name. She threw the best holiday parties and always had a reputation for being a collector. Her old Victorian-style house was like a museum of ancient trinkets and kitsch. But then again, that's why so many people liked staying there.

I finished the stew and cleaned up, sinking into bed with a sigh. Tomorrow. I'd go investigate tomorrow. But for now? I needed sleep.

COLLISION COURSE

SEBASTIAN

"This is all hers?" I gaped at the pile of boxes. They reached toward the ceiling and tottered precariously.

"Well, that's most of it, anyway," Rosemary said. "You should know all about dragons. They hoard." She shrugged and gave me a good natured smile.

"Yeah," I breathed, looking around. It was going to take forever to go through everything.

"I'll give you some time alone. But if you need anything, or have any questions, please let me know. I'll be down at Town Hall for the rest of the day."

"Thanks."

"Oh, and Sebastian?" She called from the door frame,

throwing her head over her shoulder.

"Yeah?"

"Welcome home." Rosemary smiled sweetly, her eyes flashed, and then she was gone.

I stood there in the foyer, looking at the remnants of the life I'd left behind. I didn't know anything about running a Bed and Breakfast, despite having grown up in one. I didn't know anything about settling affairs of the dead, either, but here I was.

My dragon coiled inside me, squeezing at my heart. He'd been increasingly insistent ever since returning to the Valley. Probably felt the presence of so much magical energy around us. Probably wanted to come out and play.

I pressed my lips into a line and ran a hand through my hair, sighing. I found an empty chair and sunk into it. My eyes stared off into the cold, bare room.

That was two things the Dozing Dragon never was: cold, or empty. There were people passing through at all times of the year, shifters and vampires and witches and fairies and even more I didn't know how to name. The Dozing Dragon, my mother's bed and breakfast, served as a quaint little respite from the stresses of the outside world. It wasn't as glamorous as the Vale Valley Inn and

Restaurant, but it had the kind of character you can only find in small towns like these.

A warm meal, good company, and a fireplace that never went out, even on the coldest nights of winter.

But now? The fireplace was bare. Darkened. A shell of what once was.

That was her secret, after all. My mother kept the fires burning by lighting them herself with dragonfire. It burned cleaner, hotter, and longer. But now even it had fizzled out, just like her life.

I raked my eyes across the piles of boxes and the grand staircase leading up to the guest rooms. Nostalgia flowed in hot and heavy now, wrapping around me like the tides. I still couldn't believe she was gone.

Papers rustled in my lap, fluttering from a slight draft under the door. I grabbed them before they flew away. I shivered. That would be first on the list to fix.

"You have a choice," Rosemary had told me when she led me up the hill to the B&B. "Nellie's left you the Dozing Dragon. I remember when her parents owned it, and her parents before that. It would be a shame to see such a family institution die, but...," she'd paused, eyeing me, "I know you have your own life out there in the big city. It's your decision."

A decision I wasn't ready to make. I balled my hands into fists, creasing the forms in my lap. My mother's will stared up at me, sterile and legal and black and white. Not at all like my memory of her.

If I'd had once more chance... I wondered, then shook my head.

I needed to deal with the now. I stood up, paced to the other side of the room, and started moving boxes.

THE HANDS-ON WORK WAS GOOD FOR ME. IT WAS something I hadn't had much chance to do after starting the firm in New York, but it soothed me as I moved things from the house into my truck. It kept me busy. It gave me a purpose. And most of all, it kept the grief just barely at bay.

I was heading out the door with a particularly large box when I took a misstep and ran into something. Or someone.

A little squeak erupted from in front of me and I stumbled, nearly dropping the box. I managed to catch it just in time.

"Oh, I'm so sorry!" The voice gasped.

I tried to peer over the box, but it was too large to see much of anything. With a huff, I propped it on the outstretched windowsill and got a good look at who I'd just run into.

Well, steal my scales. that was Will Sterling.

"Sebastian?" Will asked, his eyes wide. "When did you..." He stumbled over his words, face turning red. "I was just coming up here to see if..."

He looked past me and his face fell. "She's really gone."

I nodded my head slowly, fighting the lump in my throat. "Yeah. So sudden, too. They say she went peacefully, though. No pain."

"God..." Will breathed. "She was one of my best customers. I just made a delivery up here not three days ago. If I would have known..."

"None of us could have known," I said, but it came out a little harsher than I intended. My shoulders drooped.

I remembered Will from growing up here. He'd come to town only a couple years before I left, but something about him always managed to catch my eye. I knew he was an omega, could smell it all over him, but besides that? I knew nearly nothing. He'd always been so shy. Didn't let anyone in.

And now he was standing in front of me, older and stronger and, well, irritatingly adorable, if I had to admit it. Sparks burned in my chest as my dragon woke, circling my heart.

There was something about him, all right. Even if I couldn't put my finger on it yet, I wanted to know more.

After I dealt with my mom's affairs, of course. I sighed and looked back to the pile of boxes still in the living room. Gods, when did she get so much *stuff*?

"I can help," Will offered, sidestepping me to enter the house. "It's the least I could do."

I started to protest. "I appreciate it, but—"

"No buts. I'm helping. Now where do these boxes go?"

I HAD TO ADMIT, THE JOB GOT DONE TWICE AS FAST with an extra set of hands. But the longer I stayed around this omega, the more my body and soul started to react to him. Not to mention my dragon. It paced anxiously in my chest, nagging me to make a move. I didn't dare.

This was probably the worst time ever to try dating someone. With business matters in the air back in New York and the fresh loss of my mother? I had my mental and emotional hands full. Adding the complexity of a relationship was not in the cards.

No matter how good he smelled, or how I glanced at his tight little ass when he bent over...

I shook my head. I had a job to do here, and that job wasn't mooning over this random omega. I needed to clean up the old house, move mom's stuff into storage, and figure out the fate of the B&B. Selling it seemed like the obvious choice. More money for me, and less ties to the place I'd left behind.

I left Vale Valley for a reason, I reminded myself. And no matter how charming it was, I'd made a name for myself elsewhere. It would be foolish to give all that up now.

"I think that's everything," Will said from behind me, startling me out of my thoughts. His cheeks were rosy with exertion and cold, his breath coming out in little puffs of mist. I resisted the urge to wrap my arms around him and chase the cold away.

After all, I could. I was a dragon.

FIRESIDE CHAT

SEBASTIAN

*W*ill rubbed his hands together. Even though we were inside, I could still see each puff of his breath. The Dozing Dragon was dead cold, lifeless without its owner.

I'd been careless, not stoking the flames first thing. As a dragon shifter, I naturally ran a bit hotter than humans. I hadn't expected anyone else to show up. Certainly not this delicious omega.

"Let me get a fire started," I told him. "You're shivering." My voice dropped as I said that. Couldn't help but imagine what it would be like to take him into my arms. To warm him. To claim him.

Despite every resistance, the magical energy of Vale Valley flowed around me and through me. I was more than just a human. I was more than a business-minded robot. I was a shifter, and my primal nature was starting to come out.

To tell you the truth? That scared me.

I busied myself with the fireplace to take my mind off the omega in my living room. It had been burning as long as I could remember, sustained by my mother's magical dragonfire. Now it was dead, and so was she. I bit my lip, wondering if I could call up enough fire to light it again.

I tried. I reached down within me, to that part of my soul I'd so long neglected. Got nothing but sparks on my tongue and a smoky taste on my breath. Figures.

"Something wrong?" Will asked me. He stood by the Christmas tree, gazing at the lavish decorations. It seemed almost out of place in this cold, bare room. A relic of a bygone time where the hearth flickered with life and a hot meal was always around the corner.

I cleared my throat. "Out of firewood," I muttered, shaking my head. "Gotta go gather some."

Will peeled back one of the curtains, eyes wide. "You can't really be thinking about going out there right now, snow's blowing everywhere!"

I looked. He was right. A cold wind howled through the skeletal trees, their branches bowing. We'd been warned about this blizzard, but I thought it wasn't supposed to come in for another day. Guess I was wrong.

In the last waning rays of daylight, a white fog blustered across the landscape, obscuring all in its path. The sunset painted the small, sleepy valley in rich hues of amber and gold. Each ray of light was a glistening diamond on ice.

Was it cold? Yes. But I was struck with something else as I watched the gale of Mother Nature rush around us. It was beautiful. It was powerful. And something about that called to me in the deepest part of my soul. I had to go.

"I'll be fine," I assured Will and turned for the door.

"But you're not even wearing a coat!" He cried, rushing forward to grab my hand. His skin was cold as ice, sending prickles of not just cold but surprise and desire racing up my arm and straight to my dragon. He stirred and paced, a warm roar bubbling through me.

My eyes flashed gold and the world sharpened around me. Each speck of dust, each reflection of light off the baubles and ornaments on the tree. Each sliver of ash in the deadened fireplace. I turned to Will and placed my hands on his shoulders. I caught those beautiful eyes and held them there, suspended for the briefest moment in time.

"Sebastian?" Will asked, his voice weak. "The fire?" He nodded to the still chilly room and the empty hearth.

"Oh." I drew back like I'd been shocked. I cleared my throat and turned my face away so he couldn't see the fiery blush heating my cheeks. The firewood. The mission. Right.

I shook my head and squeezed my eyes tight. I'd almost lost control there. Too close for comfort. I should send Will on his way home. This was no place for a lone omega. And yet...

"Stay here," I rumbled. "I'm coming back for you."

Still shocked at the intensity of my own words, I opened the door and stepped out into the blizzard.

THE ICY GALE PUSHED AGAINST ME AND I SQUINTED my eyes, trying to see through the whiteout. No use. Will was right, it was a mess out here. But if I couldn't start a fire, then what good was I?

Some dragon I'd turned out to be.

I froze, realizing I'd heard that in my mother's voice. Great. I was even disappointing her in death. I clenched my fists, set my jaw, and moved forward.

Dragons may run a little hotter than humans, but that isn't to say that we don't get cold. By the time I'd found enough dry wood for the fireplace, I was wet, sore, and frozen to the bone. Not even my considerable insulation could make up for the chill that wormed its way through me.

Maybe, the voice in my head chided, *if you hadn't been trying to be all alpha and come out here without a coat, you wouldn't be in this predicament right now.*

Ugh.

I hefted the wood under one arm and started stomping back toward the house. When I drew closer I noticed lights on from within, and a figure moving around from behind the curtains.

He'd stayed.

Something about that touched me, just then. What reason did he have to stay in this cold old house waiting for me? It was blustery and cold, sure, but if he'd really wanted to? He could have left, no problem. Vale Valley Inn and Restaurant would have a roaring fire this time of night, as would just about every other establishment in the Valley.

So the question remained...why?

The voice within me, the voice of my dragon, thought he had an answer to that.

Because he's yours.

The door banged against the hinges the moment I touched it. Wind and dead leaves and snow blew into the house in a wet, stormy torrent. I threw myself inside and shoved the door closed, having to put all my weight behind it.

The door latched, and the house fell silent again.

That could have gone better. Now I had a whole pile of slush and leaves to clean up as well. I kicked off my boots and shook the snow out of my hair. I was still freezing, but at least I was out of the wind. I'd warm up a lot quicker than Will would, which made starting the fire all the more important.

I'd gone scavenging just in time. The sun set low on the horizon now, a final pale strip leaking over into our world. In just another few moments, night would arrive once more. Though the sky was full of clouds and blowing snow, I could still see a razor-thin sliver of the moon watching over us.

And that soothed the shifter inside me.

Even though I tried my best to find dry wood, the fact was, nothing was totally dry out there right now. I hoped they would still light.

That, or that I'd have to figure out how to use my dragonfire.

My phone buzzed in my pocket but I ignored it. My hands were too full.

I walked by the large kitchen with my arms full of firewood and caught the smell of something sweet. It brought back memories instantly—cups of hot cocoa on a cold night. Whipped cream. Sweaters and blankets and steaming mugs.

I poked my head into the kitchen. Will snapped his head up to greet me, a smile on his face. He stood over the stove, stirring a pot of something that looked suspiciously like my mom's special cocoa recipe.

"Thought you could use a warm drink," Will offered. He ladled the warm liquid into a mug and held it out toward me. "Go get the fire started, I'm almost done."

I stood there for a few moments, staring at him. Not

only had he not left, but he'd taken it upon himself to start up the stove and make cocoa.

Damn, I wasn't trying to fall in love, but this omega sure was making it easy. My mouth opened and closed a couple of times before I found the words. "You didn't have to..."

Will just waved me away and turned back to the stove. "Go on, don't get dirt in the cocoa! I'll be right there."

I walked out of the kitchen in a daze, still enjoying the warm scent of chocolate in the air and the fresh pine boughs over the hearth. The wood didn't take long to pile up and after a few false starts, the wood was hissing, sizzling, and popping. Finally, the last of the moisture burned away and flames tickled at the logs, flickering up toward the chimney. I'd just taken a step back to admire my handiwork when Will entered the room with two mugs on a tray.

Will set the tray on the table and pulled up a chair next to the fireplace. I joined him and couldn't help watching his quick, efficient movements. He'd always kind of reminded me of a small animal, even before I left town. Like a rabbit, maybe. Small, skittish, ready to run off at a moment's notice. But he wasn't running. Why was that?

"Oh hey!" Will called, brightening. "You've got wood!"

"I've—wha—" I dropped my hands to groin level, heart racing. I spun on my heel and just about ran out of the kitchen.

Then Will laughed. And what a laugh it was. Didn't matter that I was totally mortified and my dragon was doing somersaults. I could listen to the music of his voice forever.

"Oh my god!" Will cried between choking laughs. "The firewood! For the hearth! What did you think I was talking about?" His eyes danced with amusement and his body shook with each laugh.

Oh. OH. I started laughing too, and once I started I couldn't stop. It was ridiculous. Everything about this situation was ridiculous. I was back in Vale Valley, there was a strange omega in my mom's kitchen, and I "had wood"...in more ways than one.

I'd been through so much stress. So much grief. I hadn't even had a chance to process it all properly. So what could I do? I laughed. I let it all go, and I laughed.

I stared into the mug for a few moments, letting the steam hit my face and the warmth of the mug unfreeze my hands. The fire had picked up now, and was roaring away merrily in the hearth. The flames threw long shadows through the room and the warm, cozy odor of burning wood. It wasn't able to change colors like my mom's fire, but it was good enough for now.

"Oh, one more thing." Will fished into his pockets. "A little sweet treat."

He handed me a candy cane.

There were those memories again. The smells, sounds, tastes of the holidays in Vale Valley. My mom's smile. Her laugh. I hadn't even been here a day, and already this place was working its magic on me. The cold walls of ice I'd built around my heart were starting to melt, little by little. And I didn't know what I was gonna do when they were gone.

I met Will's eyes and reached forward to take the peppermint from him. Our fingers brushed for the briefest moment, and I jerked my hand away as a spark passed between us. Will's eyes lit up with the same shock. He wiped his hand on his pants, looking away.

"Must be static," he mumbled, suddenly very interested in his cocoa.

Right. Static.

Mate! My dragon screeched inside me. *Mine! Mine!*

I closed my eyes, wanting to remember this scent forever. The crackling of the hearth. The smell of the hot steamy cocoa. The fresh scent of pine. And then there was something else, hidden beneath it all. The delicious, spicy scent of cinnamon.

I opened my eyes, looked around. It was coming from him. From Will. If cinnamon wasn't my favorite flavor before, well...it was now. I buried my face in my mug and took a few sips, trying to squelch the flood of sensations rushing over me. Surely I wasn't the only one that was feeling this. I couldn't be.

But I stayed the course. Sipped my cocoa. And watched as the fireplace danced before us.

SUPERSTITIONS

WILL

*J*could have left. Hell, I probably should have left.

Yet I was here, wondering if the Dozing Dragon really was magical after all.

And what was that spark that had passed between us?

I'd hastily brushed it off. Told him it was static electricity, nothing more. But the way my heart raced, the way my soul sung out for him? I knew that wasn't the case.

It was almost like I was meant to find him here. Like I was meant to get stuck in the snow with this grumpy alpha. Like I had a part in all of this, somehow. Some way.

When I'd walked up the hill to check on the Dozing Dragon, I hadn't actually expected the spirits to be telling the truth. But there it was. The sign on the door saying 'closed for business', and Nellie nowhere to be found.

Only, I'd found something else instead.

Her son.

I remembered him vaguely from my first years here in the Valley. I hadn't really taken a chance to get to know anyone, back then. I was still in survival mode after escaping from my old town. Seeing ghosts and hearing voices? Anywhere but here, that was liable to get you thrown in the hospital. Or worse.

Even here, with all the magic and diversity around us, I still held on to some of those lingering fears. I'd learned well enough that if I ever showed my true self, nothing good would come of it. So I didn't. I kept to myself. Ran my little flower shop. Kept busy.

Until I ran right into Sebastian, and everything changed.

I took a breath and decided to try to make conversation. Anything to cut through this awkward silence. "So how was it, after you left the Valley?" If there was one thing I'd learned from staying here, it was that most people didn't leave. They either grew up here, or found the place when they needed it most. But I remembered Sebastian making the announcement that he was leaving for business school in the big city. It was quite a big deal, back then, for one of us to go back into the human world. But I knew, even back then, that this alpha had greater ambitions than Vale Valley. I admired that, in a way. Even had a little bit of a crush on him before he left.

Not that I ever did anything about it, of course. He was destined for so much more than a shy little omega like me.

But now he was here, and we were sitting in front of Nellie's fireplace with hot cocoa and candy canes and a glittering tree watching us.

Like every cheesy holiday movie ever, I grinned at the thought.

"Different," Sebastian said, reclining back into the plush armchair. He put his feet up on an ottoman and regarded me over the rim of his mug. "I grew up here, you know. Didn't know what it was like."

"And wanderlust got a hold of you?" I offered.

Sebastian smiled. I could get used to that. "Something like that."

"I heard you're doing pretty well for yourself."

He took a few moments to answer this time, regarding his cocoa with ferocious intensity. "I stay busy," he said finally. "Was actually in the middle of closing a huge deal right before I got the news."

"Oh." My heart sank. Of course he had a life outside the Valley. There were people that depended on him. It was foolish to think that he would stay.

And yet, my heart yearned for just that.

"You'll be heading back up to New York, then?" I asked. I already knew the answer.

Sebastian paused for a moment, pursing his lips in thought. His eyebrows knitted together, forming a deep crease on his forehead. "Yeah," he said at last. "I've got work to do."

"And the Dozing Dragon?" My voice shook. I couldn't help it. "It's yours now, by law. What are you going to do with it?"

This time the alpha didn't answer. Tension clouded between us, neither one of us willing to make the next move. My heart was sinking, and something deep inside me wailed with the loss of something I'd never even had.

He was leaving. He didn't care about this place. Didn't care about the Valley.

Don't get attached, I told myself through gritted teeth.

Too late, came the voice from inside me.

"Hey," Sebastian spoke up after what seemed like forever. He drained his mug and set it back on the tray. "I can probably stay until the Festival of Fire, at least. It was always my favorite part of the season."

My face fell. He didn't know. And I didn't know how to tell him.

"Seb," I started, liking the way the nickname felt on my tongue. "We...we haven't had the Festival in years. There was a fire, and someone died, and..." I stared at the ground, trying to ignore the lump in my throat. "We haven't had the heart to do it since."

Not just someone, I reminded myself. The one person who'd taken me in when I first got to the Valley with nothing more than the clothes on my back.

Sebastian's eyes widened. His face fell and yet another shadow of grief passed over him. I shouldn't have said anything. First to lose his mother, and then the Festival...

"Jesus," Sebastian muttered. "I didn't know."

"It's okay," I whispered. "You couldn't have."

Because you abandoned your home, was what I couldn't voice.

And so we sat there, watching the flames and dreaming of better days.

I WAS WALKING DOWN A LONG CORRIDOR. IT LOOKED like the ones in the Dozing Dragon, but different somehow. Like the house had gained a mind of its own and started shifting things around. I kept walking, but still the endless hall stretched out before me. What did it mean?

"Hello?" I called into the darkness. I didn't really expect an answer. But one came.

A ghostly figure floated out of the wall just in front of me and I jumped backward in surprise. No matter how many times I saw them, they always startled me. Stupid ghosts, just popping up whenever they felt like it! The whole 'coming out of the walls' thing was kinda hard to get used to, as well.

The ghost turned to face me and I swear my heart must have stopped dead in my chest.

That was no ordinary ghost. That was Nellie Wallace, former proprietor of the Dozing Dragon. Sebastian's mother.

The spirits I saw usually were random passersby. No one I knew. But this was definitely Nellie, and if she was here, that meant she had a message for me.

"It's good to see you again, dear," she said, her voice just like it had been in life, if a little more tenuous.

"What are you doing here?" A shiver rocked through me from head to foot.

"I've got a job for you, boy." She grinned that Cheshire Cat grin, and snapped her fingers. In an instant, everything went black and the chime of a grandfather clock echoed in my ears.

"Wha?" I mumbled, snapping awake. The chimes continued, and I realized they were coming from Nellie's old clock she kept in the den. I peered with blurry, sleep-riddled eyes toward it.

Midnight.

I must have fallen asleep. Rubbing my eyes, I tried to get my bearings. I was in the Dozing Dragon. There were two empty cocoa mugs on the tray beside me. And where did this blanket come from?

I picked at the soft, woolen hand-knit. I didn't remember any blanket before I fell asleep.

And that meant...

Thoughts came back to me now, filling in the gaps.

I'd come here to check on Nellie. But Nellie was dead. Instead, I found her son, returned from New York to deal with his mother's affairs.

Sebastian.

Even thinking the name sent a shiver of need through my body. I had always been good at falling for the wrong people, but this took the cake. There was nothing between us. I'd helped him out of respect for Nellie, that was all.

But it isn't, the little voice in the back of my mind whispered. *You want him.*

And this was far from the first time I had wanted something I couldn't have.

He'd be done with this place soon enough, and jet back to New York City with his big skyscrapers and fancy suits. He'd chosen that life, and who was I to tear him away from it?

I tossed the blanket aside and stood up, bracing for a moment on the side of the chair until I got my balance. Sebastian was nowhere to be seen, and the house was so big and labyrinthine I probably couldn't find him if I tried. Instead, I focused on the next step in front of me.

I'd imposed long enough. It was time to leave.

I flipped on the porch light and peered out the chilly windows. The wind and snow had let up, finally, and the town hung suspended in the quiet embrace of winter. Snow drifts pressed against trees and down the road sloping toward the center of town, but the storm had passed.

Who knew when it would return again, so I grabbed my coat off the hook and made for the door.

"Will?" The voice called.

At first, I thought it was another spirit playing tricks on me. But then I recognized that voice. That was Sebastian.

I followed the source of the sound down a long hallway not unlike the one in my dreams. I turned a corner and there he was, hunched over a desk with a notebook and laptop by his side.

He turned to face me. "You're awake." There was no surprise there. Simply stating the facts. I looked beyond him and saw a spreadsheet filled with numbers and graphs on his screen. Even in the dead of night, he just couldn't stop working.

"I was trying to be quiet," he added, shifting in his seat.

"You didn't wake me." I shook my head. "But I think I need to go. It's late."

Sebastian tilted his head. "Now? It's the middle of the night."

"Weren't you just trying to get rid of me earlier?" I teased, remembering how he'd tried to shoo me away when I first arrived.

That silenced him.

"Besides," I added. "The storm has let up at last. I wanna get out of here while I still can."

Seb's eyes flashed with something I couldn't name. Loneliness? Loss? It was gone in an instant, and he regained his steely demeanor. "If that is your wish," he said, and then added, "Thank you, Will. For the help today."

I tried to ignore the tugging at my heart. The singing in my soul. Dammit, I wanted him more than I'd ever wanted an alpha before, and it was that much worse because I knew I couldn't have him. I had to get out of here while I still had my sanity.

"I'm sorry," I muttered. "Thanks for everything, but I've really got to go."

I turned and walked back down the hallway, cursing myself at every step. This was for the best. It had to be.

I was standing under the doorway when I heard footsteps behind me.

"Wait," Seb called out. I froze, and a tiny spark of hope flared within me. What was it now?

I turned around and he was standing there, watching me. Those gold flecks in his eyes were brighter than ever, watching me with an intensity that both unnerved and aroused me.

"What?" I crossed my arms, and then I happened to notice what was hanging right above me.

Mistletoe.

You have *got* to be kidding me.

It all came back to me now. In fact, I was the one that *made* this delivery. Nellie always wanted all the seasonal plants for the holidays, so I'd delivered several wreaths along with holly, poinsettias, and—oh, right—mistletoe. Never mind the fact that we had very strict guidelines for handling it. It was known to trigger heats in unmated omegas, and none of us wanted to deal with that on the job.

But now, standing in front of this alpha with his lingering scent calling me closer? I almost hoped it would.

"Huh," I said, a nervous laugh coming out. "Would you look at that." I pointed upward.

"Oh, the mistletoe?" Sebastian asked. His eyes flashed golden once more. "What about it?"

I sputtered.

"Mom was into all those superstitions." Seb shrugged.

I raised an eyebrow. "Superstitions?" I repeated. "Come on, man. Everyone knows the meaning of mistletoe. When we get it into the shop, it even comes with special instructions on handling it. Quite the naughty plant, depending on who you ask. Some of the old witches here use them for fertility treatments, I think. They call it the Life-Giver."

I was blushing just saying that. Why did he care? And

why did I suddenly feel rooted to the spot, unable to think or breathe?

"Legends," Sebastian said dismissively, waving his hand. "Nellie was full of them. I've dedicated my life to reason, not magic."

"What are you implying?" I asked, cocking my hip out to one side. The hairs on the back of my neck stood on end, and suddenly I felt feisty. I didn't know why I was challenging him on this when I was supposed to be hightailing it back home, but something pressed me forward.

"It doesn't work," the alpha repeated, crossing his arms. "Old wive's tales."

"Oh yeah?" I retorted, flaring my nostrils. "Prove it."

Then Sebastian advanced on me like a predator stalks his prey. He never took his eyes off mine and as he closed the distance between us, he growled.

"Maybe I will."

MIDNIGHT MISTLETOE

WILL

The heat of Sebastian's lips on mine took my breath away. I leaned into the kiss, tilting my head upward to reach him. There was that low, growling sound again, and Seb brought me closer, wrapping a hand around my waist. I knew I should go. Leave.

But his scent overwhelmed me, made me forget myself. And the mistletoe hung above us, watching our every move. The connection between us heightened and this time when we kissed, sparks literally flew. Like kissing a firecracker. All smoke and wood and earthy, delicious scents I could lose myself in...

Maybe I already had.

"You okay?" Sebastian rumbled, moving his lips closer to

my ear. His tenor echoed through me and I shivered, my skin popping up in gooseflesh.

"Yeah," I whispered. But that wasn't even the half of it. The mistletoe had ignited my lingering desire and curiosity, turning into a full blown inferno. My skin tingled all over, impossibly sensitive. Sweat gathered on my forehead, and the room was way too hot...

"No fucking way," Seb growled when he realized what was happening. "You're not..."

"Told you," I panted, looking up into those golden eyes.

He paused for a moment, his lips only inches away from my jawline. I could feel the heat spilling off of him and it was almost too much to bear. I needed him...all of him. Now.

"If we do this," Sebastian whispered in my ear, "there's no going back. You understand that, right?"

My knees turned to jelly at his words and I sagged against him, every cell in my body crying out for his touch. "Please, alpha," I whined. "Claim me."

That definitely got a reaction out of him. Seb dug his nails into my back and pulled me ever closer, dragging his lips and teeth across my jawline, my neck, my shoulder. He reached the sensitive gland there and nuzzled it, drawing in my scent.

"You smell," he groaned, taking another sniff, "so fucking good." He ran his tongue along the path between my neck and shoulder, then sucked the flesh into his mouth like a hungry animal.

I moaned and arched against him, my mouth opening wide in a silent exclamation of pleasure. Endorphins and adrenaline shot through my body, lighting up every sensitive area I had, and some I didn't even know about.

"So do you believe me now?" I breathed, a husky laugh bubbling free. I gave him a teasing glance and he claimed my lips again. He wasn't gentle this time. Far from it. Like a starving man at a buffet, he wanted not only to taste, but to devour.

And may I be damned, but I wanted him to. The hunger grew and coiled inside me as I ground my hips into his. I was hard already, achingly so, and every bit of friction only stoked the flames higher.

Sebastian pulled away at last, panting. A wide, giddy smile stretched across his face. "Maybe there is something to those stories after all."

I couldn't help but smirk. I loved it when I was right.

And I loved it even more when that meant Seb was kissing me.

Sebastian ran his hands across my chest, down toward my waist and around to cup the curve of my ass. I gasped, desperate for more.

"Wha-what are you doing?" I breathed. I watched wide-eyed as he went to his knees in front of me.

"They never say what you have to kiss under the mistletoe."

And there he was, working at the buckle on my pants, unzipping them, pulling them down around my legs. I threw my head back in a sigh. I couldn't believe this was happening. Or rather, I could...but it was happening to *me*.

And the one alpha I'd had a silly crush on years ago was pulling down my pants, a feral hunger glittering through his every movement.

Gods, this was too good to be true.

I hissed and wound my hands into Seb's hair, mewling despite myself. Everything was so hot, so needy, so...

I opened my eyes and looked down at my alpha as my cock sprung free.

So *mine.*

Seb kneeled like a man praying in front of me, only this time he wasn't worshipping any god. He was worshipping my cock.

His warm, gentle hands trailed a path from my belly down the smattering of hair leading to my crotch. I shivered at the touch, so light and gentle, and so not enough. I wriggled and moaned, thrusting toward him.

"What are you—" I breathed again, my thoughts hazy.

"Patience, little one. Anticipation is half the fun."

At that, I growled. A sound I didn't even know I could make. Seb's eyes flicked to mine and went full gold. The last of my resolve shattered and I melted into him as the pieces clicked together.

Of course he was.

"You're a dragon," I said in wonder. "Just like your mom."

A deep, husky rumble erupted from his chest at that. Hot breath enveloped my cock. "I am. And my dragon wants you."

"What about you?" I managed to get the words out. "Do you want me?" My last sliver of sense told me to be wary, to be careful. If I mated with the wrong alpha, there was, as Seb had said, "no going back."

But the fear didn't take long to subside. I didn't believe it. Not really. The way my soul sung out for him, the way my body reacted to his every touch...mistletoe or no, this had to be fate.

"More than words can say," Sebastian growled, and then he took me into his hot, waiting mouth.

The sensation nearly drove me over the edge at once, all-consuming and intense. I moaned and bucked against him, grabbing the door frame for support as my knees weakened. Seb held me steady, his hands (or were they claws?) keeping me close. Protected. Safe.

His.

"God," I cursed with a hand in his hair. "That feels so fucking good."

He lapped out his tongue across my length (god, was it that long before?) and teased the sensitive head, all while suckling me down to the base of my cock. The intensity flared and continued, reducing me to nothing but a mewling, bucking mess.

Then the dragon made a sort of humming sound, deep in his chest. His mouth vibrated around my cock, delivering sensation after sensation of sweet, hot pleasure. I gasped and held on for dear life, clinging to my dragon as orgasm hit me. "Seb!" I cried, digging my nails into his shoulders and holding him against me. "Fuck!"

Hot, messy cum spurted between us and that impossibly agile tongue took it all, every last drop.

I sagged bonelessly against him, totally spent.

"I'm not done with you yet."

Neither am I, sung the voice in my mind.

Sebastian kicked my discarded pants to the side and grabbed my hand. His skin was still blisteringly hot, searing into me like a brand. I didn't care. If it was with him, I wanted to burn.

"Come on," he muttered, pulling me away from the door. We walked hand in hand through the living room and down the hallway. I knew where we were heading immediately.

Was sex with a dragon always like this? I wondered deliriously before Seb pushed me into a bedroom and shut the door. I landed on the bed and bounced, watching Seb with lust-crazed eyes. Even though I'd just come, it did nothing to still the fire inside me. The fire he'd placed there, like he'd reached all the way down to my soul and lit me up from the inside. I knew at this point only one thing would cure it. Only one thing could soothe this ache, and I needed it more than I needed air.

Seb closed and locked the door, then rounded on me, his glittering eyes raking up and down my exposed body.

"Less clothes," he growled, pulling his own shirt over his head. I followed suit and tossed my top to the side, but not before sucking in a breath at my alpha's exposed chest.

For someone who seemed to resent his shifter nature, he sure was going all out on it this time. His wide chest rippled with muscles and just a smattering of hair, but that wasn't what caught my eye. Thin, shining slashes cut across his torso and arms like fiery tattoos.

That is, if tattoos could move.

They swirled and danced across his skin effortlessly, showing through to the fire within. I couldn't tear my eyes away, and to my surprise, neither could Sebastian.

"What is that?" I asked, my voice low. The fire curled across his arms now, then up to his neck. They left tendrils of light in their wake.

Sebastian shook his head, glaring at the markings on his arms. "I...I don't know. I've heard things, but this..."

"Does it hurt?" I asked. Each line of fire slashed across his skin like a brand, burning him from the inside out.

"No, actually," Sebastian said, flexing his arms. The symbols moved and danced with him, uncannily alive. "It feels...wow, I don't even know. It's good. I know that much."

He held out his hands to me. "Don't be afraid."

I was...a little, but it was the good kind of fear. The kind where you know something amazing is just on the other side. The connection between us could not be denied. I placed my hands in his, and the fire crossed over between us. I nearly flinched away as I watched it come, but he was right. It didn't burn me. Instead, it felt like it was unlocking something inside of me. Drilling down to the deepest parts of my being, where not even I had ventured before.

"I think it means we're mates," Sebastian breathed.

"I think you're right," I replied, and buried my face in his chest.

His heartbeat thrummed there, steady and strong. It cried out to me and struck a chord. Our heartbeats were one, thudding along at the same time as the rest of the world spun around us. I'd never felt anything like it in my whole life, and knew that I never would again. This was it for me.

This was my mate.

"Alpha," I sighed into him. "Please."

"Tell me what you want, Will," Sebastian said as he stroked my hair. "What you need. I'd give you the moon if you asked me."

"You." The word broke free before I could think about it. "All of you. In me. Around me. Please, I'm burning up, I'm..."

"I'm here, Will." He punctuated the words with kisses. "I'm here, darling. I'll take care of you." Sebastian nuzzled the gland at my neck again, filling me up with his scent. "Relax," he rumbled, and this time I wasn't even sure he'd spoken aloud.

I melted around him, arching my hips forward to meet his. Our cocks met and rubbed against one another. A shower of sparks rolled down my spine and I fisted the sheets, hissing. It wasn't enough. Could never be enough, not until—

"Lift up your legs," Sebastian growled. "I need to see you."

I pulled my legs toward my chest and sucked in a breath. My tight, aching ass was wet with slick and throbbing with need. Right in front of his cock.

Seb dipped a hand below my waist and a deep, satisfied rumble echoed through my bones. "Yessss." He drew out the word while swiping a finger against my crease. I bit my lip and twisted against him, the need nearly driving me crazy. If I didn't have him in me soon, I'd surely lose it.

"One last chance, omega." Sebastian watched me with golden irises. "Tell me what you want."

"Claim me, Sebastian. I'm yours, I'm yours!" I didn't care how ridiculous I sounded anymore. I just knew I needed to soothe that delicious ache, or I'd never be the same again.

He didn't need any more convincing than that. I watched as his eyes flashed from golden to reptilian slits, his skin breaking out in a rough pattern of scales.

"Fuck, I'm shifting!" Seb cried in a ragged tone.

"Now!" I screeched, and my alpha buried his cock all the way inside me.

I'd never felt so full in all my life. Sebastian's hard length speared through me and despite the tiny prick of pain on entry, there was something much stronger in its place —a feral, all-consuming pleasure. And the feeling that this was right. So right.

I let out a shaky sigh, clawing my hands into his back. I loved the feel of his flesh under my fingertips and apparently Seb did too, because he followed suit. He not only dug into me with his cock, but with his nails as well, leaving long red stripes on my ass.

I cried out and bucked toward him, high on the sensations. It felt like flying. My alpha pounded into me, each thrust more forceful than the last. This was no tender mating, no. But I wouldn't have had it any other way. Our most primal natures had taken over, and now they were calling the shots. Rational thought had fled out the window long ago. I mewled and moaned and scratched and bit. Seb gave as good as he took, sending me higher with each delicious thrust.

"What...what is that?" I moaned, when I felt a series of ridges pressing against my prostate.

"Dragon dick," Seb said with a wink. "Ribbed for his pleasure." He rubbed against me again, as if to prove a point.

"Fuck," I groaned. "If you don't stop doing that I'm gonna—"

"Oh, what was that?" Seb teased, working that spot harder. He knew exactly where to touch me, exactly where to fuck me...like we weren't two beings at all, but one and the same. "You're gonna what?"

I squeezed my eyes shut, sparks of light flashing before my eyes. The pressure built, and built, and built...

"I'm gonna cum!" I wailed, and the pressure sent me over the edge, tumbling and free-falling toward an earth-shaking climax.

"Fuck, Will," Sebastian panted, angling his hips upward now. "You came without me even touching your cock."

"Mmhm," I whined, grabbing the fleshy globes of his ass. I pulled him into me faster, harder. Something was growing, something out of both of our control...

"Ahh, I'm gonna knot, Will," Seb leaned over and whispered into my ear, his stubble tickling my face. "I'm gonna fill you up with my seed, baby. Gonna knot you, gonna mate you..."

He thrust into me one last time, harder than ever before. With a final cry, he sunk his teeth into my shoulder, joining us together. Pain ripped through me but pleasure, too, mingling and merging until I couldn't quite tell where I ended and he began. His knot swelled and locked within me, giving me burst after burst of his cum.

The world slowed and seemed to stop around us. The cares of the outside world didn't matter, floated away. Right here, right now, I was with my mate. And nothing could touch us.

Nothing, that is, except the still-lingering fate of the Dozing Dragon.

SWEETS AND TREATS

SEBASTIAN

*E*arly morning sun filtered through the blinds, casting long slats of light on the carpeted floors. I opened my eyes slowly, trying to get my bearings. This bed was not my own. This room was facing the wrong way.

And there was a sleeping omega on the bed next to me.

I blinked, rubbed my eyes. It came back to me in a flash. For the first time in years, I'd let my dragon out to play. How could I resist, when my fated mate was right in front of me? What we'd shared together was nothing short of incredible. Just glancing at the mating bite I'd left on his skin had me getting hard all over again.

I stretched and got out of bed, checking the status of the snowstorm. Drifts and fallen limbs lay everywhere, but no more was falling and the wind had died down, for the moment, at least. From our perch atop the hill I could see people starting to move about. The colorful tents of vendors from the Christmas Market dotted the square and I heard the faint echo of music.

When in Vale Valley, right?

I turned to Will, who was just starting to open his eyes. He recognized me at once and gave me a sleepy, sated smile.

"Hey," he said, stretching like a cat in the huge bed. Then a moment of panic rushed over his face. "Wait, what day is it? I've got to get to work!"

He threw his legs over the side of the bed and started gathering up the bits of clothes we'd discarded during the night. I stood in the door way and stopped him. "Where do you think you're going, cinnabun? It's Sunday. Unless you work on Sunday."

Will blinked at me for a few moments, like his brain still wasn't awake enough to process that information, then he dropped the pile of clothes to the floor. "Wait, I thought for sure it was Monday. And Cinnabun? Seriously?"

"You smell like cinnamon." I smirked and leaned forward to grab his ass. "And I like these buns."

Will groaned. "Never say that again."

I took out my phone, pulled up the calendar and showed it to him. "It's definitely Sunday. Was the sex that good that it's messing with your memory?" I chuckled and dodged a flying sock.

"Hey!" Will yelled, chasing after me. "Come back here!"

We ended up in a laughing, bickering pile on the bed. How good it was to be around my mate this way! My dragon was more awake than I'd ever felt him, and I started to wonder what I was running from all this time. If being a shifter meant I got to feel like this, then...

"So what do you want to do today?" I asked, rolling over to face him. "Sure work's not gonna burn down without you?"

"Are *you* sure?" Will retorted. "I saw you working late last night. You can't get away from it, can you?"

I didn't expect that. Not so early in the morning, anyway. I tried to come up with words that made sense, but only found excuses. "I've worked really hard to get where I am," I said finally, knowing how pathetic it sounded. "I don't want to lose that."

Will rolled his eyes and hopped out of bed again.

"Think I can tear you away from your computer long enough for breakfast? There's this creperie downtown that's absolutely divine, and then the Market will be in full swing. You don't have to come along, but that's where I'll be." He looked at me with those wide puppy-dog eyes, though, and I knew he *did* want me to come.

I sighed and grinned up at my mate. "I guess I can take a little break. Let's see what I've been missing in the Valley these past years. Lead the way."

"Not so fast," Will pointed out. "I need to take a shower first."

He padded off to the bathroom, giving me a delicious view of his rear. "Need some company?" I called. His bare skin just begged me to touch it, love it, taste it.

"Is that even a question?" Will called over his shoulder. "Get in here."

"Welcome!"

The door chimed as we walked in, grateful for the warmth. Though the snowstorm had cleared up, the air still held a biting chill that got all the way under your coat, no matter how many layers you wore.

I shucked off my scarf and coat, hanging them on the coat rack by the door.

"You were right," I said to Will quietly, "this place smells delicious."

"Tastes even better," Will added.

It was a small, cutesy bakery with a colorful, handwritten menu board and twinkling Christmas lights hanging over the doorway. A large tree sat in the corner of the shop, completing the look.

"I'm not sure I've ever had a crepe," I admitted as I read the list. "Is it like a pancake?"

"Sort of," Will said. "Thinner. And you can add all kinds of toppings, too. What are you feeling today, sweet or savory?"

I gave him a look. "Sweet, duh."

Will grinned. "Good choice. All the options for the sweet crepes are on the left side of the menu there. Let me know if you want a recommendation. I might come here a little too often." He laughed nervously, patting his stomach.

Talk about being spoiled for choice. There were no less than ten different options on the sweets menu, and that wasn't even counting their savory offerings.

Each one of them looked more delicious than the last.

Finally, I reached the counter. Time to choose.

A cashier peered at us from behind the register with a huge grin. "See anything you like?"

"I'll have the banana and nutella crepe special, please. With whipped cream on the side."

"Excellent, that's one of our most popular items."

"It's my first time here, so good to know I've made the right choice."

"Well, welcome on in! Haven't seen you around the Valley before. You new?"

"Something like that," I muttered.

He whisked off to prepare my order and I raised an eyebrow at Will. "How'd I do?"

"Great," Will said. He slipped his hand into mine. "'S cold," he muttered, shivering. Those small fingers were like icicles!

I squeezed his hand tighter, trying to send him some of my natural warmth. It was a crime for my mate to be cold, and I made a commitment right then that he'd never have to worry about that around me. I had more than enough heat for the both of us.

"Here we are!" The cashier called, returning from the strange round contraption with a beautifully plated crepe. "One banana and nutella, with whipped cream on the side. Anything else I can get for you today? Coffee?"

"Coffee would be wonderful," I admitted. I slipped an extra dollar across the counter.

"Coming right up!"

"Well, how's your first crepe?" Will asked, watching me over his mug. He'd opted for hot tea this morning. Peppermint, by the smell of it.

I licked the whipped cream from the side of my mouth. When I saw his eyes watching me and his mouth slightly parted, I decided to make a bit of a show of it.

"Now you're jealous of my cream?" I teased, loving the way his face turned bright red. "And yes, to answer your question. It's great. Sweet. Fluffy. Rich. Pairs well with the coffee." I looked over at his plate. He'd chosen a 'strawberry surprise', whatever that was, and the crepe appeared to be completely buried beneath jam and fresh fruit. "How's yours?" I pointed at the plate with my fork.

"Awesome, as always," Will said between bites. "Wanna try some?" He held out a scrumptious-looking morsel on his fork, angling it toward me.

"Oh, sure." It looked like it packed enough sugar to make a lollipop cry, but why not?

"Open up." Will grinned. Shocked at first, I flinched away, then I realized what he was doing.

Will moved the fork toward my mouth and I closed around it, licking the utensil clean. Maybe I was just crazy, but there was something erotic about being fed by a lover. The flavors exploded on my tongue and I caught the scent of Will, as well. So close. Close enough to touch. To kiss.

So yeah. A hottie omega feeding you a strawberry crepe? Straight to the top of the public-boner list.

"Mmm," I moaned, sinking back in my chair. "That might be even better than mine." The berry explosion, rich as it looked, was surprisingly not as overwhelming as I thought it would be. The sweet flavors balanced out with the slightest citrus tang. Strawberry surprise, indeed.

"Don't get too full now," Will teased and poked my stomach. "We've got a lot of walking to do over at the Christmas Market."

"Ha," I said after another forkful of crepe. "Or we'll just have a good chance to burn off all these calories."

Will's eyes twinkled over the rim of his mug.

"I like the way you think."

WHEN WE LEFT THE CREPERIE, (TOTALLY SUGAR-high, mind you), the sun was high in the sky. Noon approached, and the sounds of the town square were audible even from here.

"God, I haven't been to a Market in..." I rubbed my forehead. "I don't even know." The longer I stayed here, the more I realized all the little things that I'd been missing out on. Vale Valley was like a weird bubble out of time. While the rest of the world ran on a non-stop pace of business, caffeine, and perpetual stress, Vale Valley seemed to have it figured out. Townspeople waved hello to one another as we passed. Some of them even remembered me, welcoming me back to the town.

In New York, that would never happen. Everyone kept to themselves and minded their own business.

Which was pretty useful if you were trying to hide the fact you were a dragon shifter, but...

"Sebastian!" A voice called from behind us. I spun around to see a young woman waving at us. It took me a moment, but when she smiled and showed those dimples on her cheeks, I knew it could only be one person.

Julia Peridale.

She ran up to us, long sleeves of her sweater trailing out behind her. "I heard the rumors, but I wasn't sure— you're back!"

"I am."

"I'm so sorry to hear about your mom. She was so good to us, for so long."

I nodded. "She was a good woman."

"Oh, and Will! I see you've taken to showing Sebastian around. Bet he barely recognizes the place anymore." She winked. "I've got to run and help my da at the kettle corn stand, but come by and see us!" She handed us both a slip of paper printed with metallic gold ink.

"Discount." She beamed. "Friends and family. Hope to see you there!"

With that, she ran off, quickly lost in the growing crowd.

"That was nice of her," Will pointed out, placing the coupon in his wallet. "You two went to school together, didn't you?"

"Primary school, yeah." It felt like so long ago. Hell, it *was* so long ago. Funny what the brain remembers sometimes.

"She's a sweetheart. I deliver succulents for her dad sometimes. He loves them."

"Sounds like you know just about everyone," I mused, looking around at the multicolored tents and stalls. Even though I grew up here, I'd never felt like more of a stranger. These people knew each other in a way that only small town neighbors could. They took the time to care for one another.

And where did that leave me? An outsider. Voluntarily, even.

Why had I left the Valley again?

I'd thought I had it all figured out. I thought I had a goal in life. A purpose.

But ever since returning to the Valley, I wasn't even sure of that anymore.

"Whoa, look at these!" Will called out, dragging me along by the hand. It took a few stumble steps to catch up with him, but I did. Will gawked at a lavishly decorated stand with garments in every color of the rainbow. There were scarves, hats, gloves, and sweaters. I even spotted a few socks.

With love in every stitch, the hand-written sign said.

"What do you think that means?" he asked, pointing to the sign.

I shrugged. "Marketing speak."

He peered closer at a flowing purple scarf, running his hands along the soft woolen stitches in awe. Maybe it was a trick of the light or a few strands of metallic yarn, but I could have sworn the fabric sparkled.

"You boys need help?" A man approached us. He sported a long ponytail, tattoos, and a tie-dyed shirt. "Made all this myself. Happy to answer any questions you have."

"Seriously?" Will said, excited. "All this? Must have taken you forever."

The man laughed. "It would using traditional methods."

He leaned in closer, dropping his voice to a conspiratorial whisper. "But my ways are not so traditional."

Both our eyes widened. Will held up the scarf, still uncannily sparkling. "Love in every stitch?"

"It is part 'marketing babble', yes," he regarded me with a pointed look, "but I'm a Tailor Mage. I can imbue my creations with different properties. Give them life they didn't have before."

This time I was the one gaping in surprise. "Whoa. I didn't—I didn't know that was a thing."

"It wasn't," the man beamed. "Till I made it one. I love fashion, and my magic kept messing things up, so I thought, why not try to combine them? Work with my talents, instead of against them?" He waved a hand around at his little shop. "And thus, Nathan's Knits was born."

"That's really cool," I said, impressed. "What does this one do, then? I could have sworn I saw it sparkle."

A knowing grin stretched across Nathan's face. "That piece there was one of my favorites to work on. Not only is it my favorite color, but I imbued silvery threads magic in there. It will always help you find your way back home."

"It's beautiful," Will cooed. "How much?"

"Well, that is part of my special collection. I put so much work into it, I'm loathe to let it go, but something tells me you two might need it more than I do. Check the price tag there on the side."

Will's face fell. "Oh. I don't have that much."

"I'll take it," I spoke up, fishing out my wallet.

"Wait, what?" Will said, astonished.

I handed Nathan the money. "Thank you, for your fine craftsmanship. And thank you for serving this Valley."

"You're welcome, sirs. Have a great afternoon, stay warm out there!"

We walked away with the scarf wrapped in kraft paper. Will caught up to me. "Hey."

"Hey."

"What was that about?"

"What?"

"You bought that for me. You didn't have to."

"You wanted it. I had the money. Simple enough to me."

"But it was—"

"It's a gift," I cut him off. "'Tis the season of giving, right?" I unwrapped it and placed it around Will's neck. "How is it?"

Will's face lights up, and something pings inside Sebastian. He'd move mountains to see that smile again. Will hugs it close, burying his face in its warmth. "It's even softer than I thought! It's...wow. Thank you, Sebastian. It's perfect."

I slipped my hand into his and we walked down the snowy path together. I still couldn't get the sight of his smile out of my mind.

Two bags of caramel kettle corn later, we were both full and tired. I'd picked up some elderberry jam and Will found saplings of a rare plant he'd been wanting to breed for the nursery. All in all, it was a good trip. But our feet were sore, our bellies were full, and our wallets were empty.

Will had started to drag, too. At first I thought it was just because he was tired, but as time wore on he began to look more and more sick. Finally, I brushed off one of the nearby benches and threw down my jacket for him to sit on.

"You okay?"

Will's face was flushed and even a little sweaty. It was nearly freezing out here and the walking was exertion, sure, but not enough to break a sweat. Will swayed a bit and grabbed onto my pant leg. I sat down next to him and wrapped an arm around his shoulder. He buried his face against me and took a breath.

"Dizzy," Will said at last. "Kinda nauseous too."

"Something you ate?" I asked, trying to stay rational. My dragon was pacing back and forth anxiously, but I needed to be the cool head in this relationship right now. "Maybe the kettle corn?"

Will rubbed his forehead and his hand came away with cold sweat. "I dunno. Don't think so."

"The crepes?" I offered.

Will furrowed his brow. "Nah. I've eaten there a million times. Never made me sick before."

"Let's get you home. Think you can make it?" I squeezed his shoulder.

"Yeah. I'm fine, just...not feeling so hot right now."

"I was getting pretty tired myself." I shrugged. "Is your place close by?"

"Fraid not." Will frowned. "The Dragon would probably be closer."

He wanted to come home with me. My mate wanted to come home with me.

"Sure you wouldn't be more comfortable at your place?" I asked, trying to keep my voice steady.

"I just wanna lay down," Will groaned.

"Dozing Dragon it is." I took his hand and helped him up. We gathered our bags and headed back up the hill toward the bed and breakfast.

Even though my mate was sick and I was worried about him, there was still something nice about bringing my omega home.

NEW DEVELOPMENT

WILL

"*Y*ou okay in there?" The voice called from the other side of the door. "Do you need anything?"

"Leave me alone," I wailed while hunched over the toilet. "I'm fine. If you wanna make yourself useful, get me some herbal tea. Peppermint."

"On it!"

I let out a sigh of relief. He was gone.

Couldn't a guy puke in peace?

I wiped my mouth and stood on shaky legs. I grabbed the bottle of mouthwash and used it to rinse, then wet a towel and hung it around my neck. I was exhausted.

What had gotten into me?

When I stepped out of the bathroom and saw Sebastian rushing about down the hall, a thought struck me. It should have been obvious. I should have known when the mistletoe triggered my heat.

I'd had sex. With an alpha. During my heat. Unprotected.

Oh, shit.

The thought nearly made me run back to the bathroom, but I kept it down. And this time, I wasn't sure if it was fear or excitement.

You might be pregnant, a little voice whined. Another ghost. Great.

You should get tested, whined another.

All of you, shut up, I mumbled, staggering toward the bedroom. I flopped onto the bed face first, burying myself in the comforter. Maybe if I just stayed here and didn't move, everything would go back to normal.

Yeah, right.

"Special delivery," Sebastian called, sidestepping me to place the tea on a tray next to the bed. Even with my head in the pillows I could smell the herbal blend.

"You're a lifesaver," I said without lifting my head. "Thank you."

The mattress sunk under me as Sebastian sat down. He placed a hand on my back, tentatively rubbing the area between my shoulder blades. "Anything else I can do?"

I rolled over and looked up at him. "I'm fine, really. And thank you for the tea."

"My pleasure. I actually just got a call from Rosemary, she wants to see me down at Town Hall. I told her it might have to wait, but if you're sure you'll be okay..."

I waved my hand toward the door. "I'm not dying, Seb. Just need to take a little breather, that's all. Go see Rosemary. Give her my greetings." I tried to give him a smile. He didn't need to know what I was worrying about right now. At least, not until it was a real problem. Right now, it was just anxiety. Nothing more.

Sebastian squeezed my hand once more and turned for the door. "I won't be long."

"Have fun," I called after him.

It wasn't until I heard the door close and the deadbolt lock that I let out a shaky breath.

What if I *was* pregnant?

I placed a hand over my stomach and maneuvered into a sitting position. The mug of hot tea steamed on the bedside table. I picked it up, warming my hands and breathing in the minty steam.

I'd never given a lot of thought to having children. After my own difficult childhood, I had enough trouble keeping myself going, much less another human being.

But I had to admit, now that I actually sat down and thought about it, there was something appealing about the whole idea. What if I had the power to create life in my very hands? What if I could raise a little one, start a family, watch them grow and learn and evolve?

My heart squeezed at the thought.

But I was getting ahead of myself. All I really knew right now was that I was feeling a little sick. And that could be from anything.

Easy enough to say. With each sip of my tea, the growing feelings of protectiveness and love washed over me. That wasn't the only thing, though. There was another: cold blooded fear and disappointment.

No matter how much I might want this, the fact remained: Sebastian wasn't staying. He was only in town to deal with the Dozing Dragon and Nellie's funeral, and that would be it.

Would the fact that we'd mated change anything? I wasn't even sure of that.

Vale Valley could never hold a big city dragon like him. And I certainly couldn't tear him away from all his accomplishments and accolades just to build a life with me.

No matter how nice that seemed.

If I was going to have a child, I'd need to take full responsibility.

I stopped, mid sip of tea, to realize how quickly I'd jumped to a conclusion.

It was too early to tell on any sort of test, even if I was pregnant. There was nothing to do now, but wait.

And see how things progressed with our still-new relationship.

I NEARLY DROPPED MY TEA WHEN AN ELDERLY woman came gliding out of the walls, stopping short when she saw me in bed. She wore a long gauzy gown and several multicolored bangles on each wrist. A jingle-bell necklace hung around her neck and sparkled with sound as she moved.

Great, what now?

"Hey," I said, not lifting my gaze.

"Oh hey," she said, turning to me. Her bangles clinked. "Haven't I seen you somewhere before?"

"Yup." A shadow passed over my face when I remembered those dark days. "You were there when Brad betrayed me and took my plans for the nursery. Remember?"

"Right. I remember that now. Wonder how he's doing these days?"

"Kicked out of town. Serves him right."

Agatha floated over to the bed and "sat" next to me. She'd been one of my only friends after my 'best friend' Brad had betrayed me, and even though she was a ghost, I treasured her company.

"And how are you doing these days?" She asked. "You're not looking so well."

I pinched the bridge of my nose. Was everyone going to make a comment about my well being today?

"I'm..." I started, then I chewed my lip, thinking. "Can I ask you something?"

"You know you can ask me anything. Us spirits see a lot

of things that humans like you can't. What's bothering you?"

I rubbed the back of my neck, not sure how to start. "There's this guy..."

Agatha nodded with a knowing grin. "There always is, sweetheart. He do you wrong again like that other boy?"

"No," I said, a little too hastily. Then, "not yet, anyway."

"And you think he will?"

I sighed and flopped backward on to the pile of pillows. "I don't know. It's all so sudden. So soon. Reminds me of what Brad did. Come in like lightning, get under my skin. Then take it all away."

"Hmm," Agatha mused. "Sounds like you're still hurting over that."

"He used me!" I cried, my voice cracking. "And when I'm with Sebastian, I get all these feelings that I'm not sure how to control and..."

"Slow down, sweetheart." Agatha placed a ghostly hand on my shoulder. It didn't feel like much, just a cold wind. I still shivered away. Ghost touches were so not my favorite, but Agatha had always been touchy feely.

"Right, sorry." She whispered, drawing away. "Now tell me, this boy of yours, he done anything to make you think he might betray your heart?"

I thought on that one. Not directly, anyway. But there was that whole matter of him moving back to New York when he was done here...

"Ah, so he's not staying," Agatha said, nodding sagely.

"I told you to stay out of my head!" I screeched, lunging toward her. She shifted out of the way just in time, and besides, it's not like I could have caught her. She was as airy as fog, impossible to hold.

Agatha simply cackled, appearing on the other side of the bed. "Sorry, sorry." She held her hands up in an 'I surrender' position. "But you're practically screaming it in your mind, I couldn't help myself..."

I sighed and grabbed a pillow, pressing it over my face.

"Why did I have to go and get mated to someone that is just going to leave me?" I said through the pillow. I didn't care that it was muffled and sounded like gibberish. Agatha would understand.

"Oh," she breathed. "Oh, honey." I didn't have to peek out from behind the pillow to know that she was looking at the mating bite on my neck.

How stupid could you get, falling prey to mistletoe and stupid Mr. Sexy Alpha? I'd totally fucked up.

"A mating is very intimate, you know. More than just quick sex."

I moved the pillow down a little. She was stretched out across the bed now, staring at the ceiling. "I remember my mate. Remember the bite like it was yesterday, too. Hurts like a bugger, doesn't it?"

I chuckled. "Yeah."

"And you want to know if you can trust this boy to stick around?"

"Yeah. I guess so. I feel like I've made the biggest mistake of my life."

Things were silent then for a few moments, the two of us sitting and watching smoke curl up from the chimneys of the neighboring houses. Snow had started to fall again, not nearly as heavily as last time, but there would definitely be a new layer on the ground by nightfall.

"You know what I do, in times like these?" Agatha said at last.

"What?"

"Listen to your heart. What does it say?"

I considered that. As cheesy and lame as it sounded, she had a point. The fear and anxiety came from that scared little boy who was bullied and betrayed. But the story of my heart said something different altogether. When I was around him, or even when I thought of him, I felt buoyed, lifted up to be more than just myself. Our bond could be something beautiful, if we let it.

If I let it.

"Thanks," I said finally. "That helps."

"Always happy to help, dear," Agatha said. She raked her eyes down my small frame one more time. "Though I still say you need some rest. Your aura is all wonky today, and I can't figure out why."

I swallowed the words on my tongue. I had an idea why, but I wasn't about to tell her. In fact, I actively tried *not* to think of it just because I knew she could detect my thoughts sometimes.

"Well, I'll leave you to your beauty rest. I've got places to be, people to haunt, all that." She grinned. "Spook ya later."

With a swirl of mist like a tiny tornado, she was gone.

AFTER CHATTING WITH AGATHA, I FELT A LITTLE better. A weight still hung over my heart, though. A weight I knew wouldn't go away until I took that damned test. How long was I supposed to wait again? I flipped through pages of info on my phone, my stomach twisting.

Was there like, a WebMD for supernaturals?

No matter what happened, I resolved as I grew tired once more, I had to protect myself first. And if there was a little one on the way? I didn't mind second place.

FIRST FLIGHT

SEBASTIAN

J was no stranger to snow. We had plenty of it in New York City this time of year. But there it was gross, gray sludge that stunk and sat around in sad, dirty piles after the plows came through.

Snow here in Vale Valley was different.

It shouldn't have been, not really. It was just frozen water, after all. But even after growing up here, it seemed there were still some secrets of the Valley I hadn't figured out yet.

It always managed to look perfectly white and fluffy, no matter how cold it got. Even the falling flakes were like feathers, brushing against my face and arms as I walked toward Town Hall.

I knew what Rosemary wanted to see me about. And I knew I wasn't ready to answer.

I tried to weigh the possibilities in my mind. On the one hand, I could just sell the Dozing Dragon, make some cash, and fly on back to NYC. Forget this ever happened, move on with my life.

But was that what I really wanted?

My dragon certainly didn't like the sound of that. He rolled around, keening. Mate, he screeched out impishly. Your mate!

And there was that.

Did I regret claiming Will there in the heat of the moment, that fateful winter night? No, that wasn't it.

But it did make things a lot more complicated. It would be harder for me to leave now, that was for sure. I had another person to look out for besides just myself, and to tell you the truth, that scared me.

I continued to let those thoughts play out, tumbling around in the back of my mind like a popcorn machine. I might not have all the answers yet, but maybe talking to Rosemary would help.

It couldn't hurt, right?

Rosemary opened the door as soon as I knocked. Almost mid-knock, actually. Like she'd known I was coming right at this moment. She probably did.

"Sebastian, come in," she greeted me. "I've got a fire going and I just got some fresh cookies delivered."

I took a long, grateful whiff. "Chocolate?"

"Why have anything else? Come on, get in here."

I stepped past her and into the Town Hall, depositing my coat on the rack by the door. Rosemary closed the door behind me and swept off down the hall, motioning for me to follow her.

I passed portraits of the Vale family and letters of recognition. There was even a sprightly wreath hung over the conference room door. The smell of cookies, hot and sweet, wafted from behind the door.

"After you."

I took my seat in one of the vinyl swivel chairs, feeling like I was in New York all over again. The long conference table, fluorescent lights, and wide windows made me think of one too many investor meetings. The hall was still rustic with that Vale Valley charm, though, and a small tree sat in the corner, blinking with lights.

I grabbed two cookies from the box at the center of the table then pushed it toward Rosemary.

"Oh no, I couldn't eat another bite. Those cookies are going to be the end of me, just watch."

I smiled and took a bite. She was right. They were perfectly warm and soft, practically melting in my mouth. They were what I liked to call 'not-quite-done', that gooey sort of half-dough, half-cookie creation you get when you take them out of the oven just a tad too early. Heaven.

"I see what you mean," I said after wiping my mouth with a napkin. "I could get addicted to those."

"I think I already have," laughed Rosemary. "But yes. We have matters to discuss."

I sat up straighter. Smoothed my shirt. Why did I feel like this was gonna be bad news?

"As you know, the Dozing Dragon has passed to you on the event of Nellie's death. I understand you need time to grieve and think it over. We all do. That's not what I mean to press you about. But we've been talking with some of the local lawyers, and they say that you'll need to make a decision on the place one way or another before the end of the month. Fiscal year technicalities, and all that. Have you given any thought to the matter?"

I blinked at her. Had I given it any thought? Hell, I'd given it pretty much *every* thought ever since coming here. I knew how much the place meant to the Valley and to my mother, but I was no Nellie. I couldn't run a B&B, even if I wanted to. I had work to go back to, and resources were tight enough as it was without having to hire on help to run the Dragon in my stead.

I sighed and rubbed my forehead. There didn't seem to be any other way out. I'd have to sell.

"Something's troubling you," she said, jerking me out of my thoughts. "Besides the usual, I mean."

I clenched my jaw and cleared my throat. She meant well, but Rosemary could be so damn nosy!

"I'm still working through our options," I said in my most business-like voice. No hint of emotion carried over. Well, maybe only a little. "You understand this would be quite a big change for me, taking over the Dragon."

Rosemary leaned back in her seat, folding her hands over her lap. "I understand." Those two words carried such disappointment I almost backpedaled right then and there.

"You're a shifter, Sebastian," she said when she found her voice again. "Magical blood runs through your veins, whether you want to admit it or not. Let it in, for once. Let it be your guide."

I grimaced and shook my head. This went against everything I'd worked for. I'd gotten out of the Valley just like I'd said I would. I became independent, successful. Free.

But what did it matter if I hurt those I loved in the process?

"There's a forest to the west of the Valley, right at the foot of the mountains. You know the one." Her eyes bored into mine and held me trapped there.

"Take some time. Clear your head. Stretch your wings, so to speak." She winked. "You'll come up with the answer you seek."

I huffed out a breath through my nose and tasted sparks. I knew she was right. Why did she have to be right? So much had happened in so little time. If I was going to figure everything out, I needed to go somewhere safe. Quiet. I needed to stop being so afraid, and let go.

I bowed my head. "I'll go."

Rosemary regarded me, clearly not done yet. "And don't think I don't know about the omega you've taken in. He's grown quite fond of you, you know."

I gulped. She really did know everything.

"You know how sacred the mating bond is. It's up to you to honor that commitment."

"I know," I said, still staring at the floor.

"Now go on," she shooed me. "And take these cookies with you! I'll eat them all if they stay here, and believe me, no one wants to see that."

"Thank you," I mumbled. "For letting me back in."

She looked affronted at that, placing a dramatic hand to her chest. "Why, it's not like we banned you or anything? You exiled yourself, Seb. I always told you, Nellie always told you, that you were free to come home whenever you wanted. I'm just sorry it took a tragedy like this to bring you back."

I winced. Harsh.

But as usual, she had a point.

"Have a good rest of your day, Rosemary." I headed for the door and donned my coat. The snow had stopped once more and the sun was even beginning to peek out from behind the wispy clouds.

"Don't forget to let me know your answer by the end of the month!" She called after me.

I breezed out into the frosty air without a word.

My mind ached. Buzzed like a hive full of bees. When did life get so complicated? I thought I had it all figured out. I had systems. I had systems for my systems. And all of this? It didn't fit into any of those boxes. Didn't play by any rules. And for the first time, I felt totally and completely lost.

I nibbled on one of the remaining cookies as I walked down the path, head down, deep in thought. It wasn't a conscious decision, but my feet started leading me west, toward the grove Rosemary recommended. I knew it well, and knew why she wanted me to go there.

It was a place I used to go with mom, just about every weekend when I was a child. Even though we lived in a civilized town, mom wanted me to know the beauty and freedom of nature. We went for regular hikes and runs. She'd point out all the birds in the sky. Every type of tree, every little herb. I thought it was all powerfully boring, back then.

But now, I'd give anything just to have her next to me one more time.

The cool air whipped through the Valley and filled my lungs, fresh and clean and full of possibility. Could I really do it?

I stretched my arms, testing the joints. I crouched, craned my neck side to side. I hadn't shifted at all in well over a decade. Thought I could lock that part of myself away. Thought it was better that way.

What had I been thinking?

The pine trees grew up around me, shielding me from the sun and snow and wind. The path grew clearer, but colder too. I walked the dimly-lit path, my feet remembering the way even when I consciously didn't.

Long nights in the meadow. My first flying lessons. Weekend picnics.

A jolt of electricity flashed through me, tingling from my fingers all the way down to my toes. My dragon swirled and paced, ready to break free. Ready to play. I blinked, my eyes shifting over from regular vision to the sharpened, vibrant colors of golden dragon eyes. Breath turned hot in my throat, a fire building from a tiny spark into an eternal flame.

I tossed the empty box of cookies aside, threw my arms out wide, and gave myself to the forest.

There it was again. That shock. That spark of light and life that wove through all shifters. It rippled through me and I hunched over, my body seizing and shaking and stretching before my eyes.

To shift from a human into an animal was no easy task. Especially when you were as big as a dragon. But I was resilient. Always had been. The pain of the shift was nothing compared to the deep, spiritual energy that released at the peak, spilling into the world around me like an orgasm. My fingers lengthened into claws. My feet grew larger, scalier. My nose picked up smells no human could, and my hearing grew attuned to every sound in the forest. I stayed hunched, curled into myself. A deep, prodding pain raced up my back and this time I didn't resist. I spread my arms, let out a breath, and raored.

Wings sprouted from my shoulder blades, wide and strong and leathery. I hadn't done this since...god, I couldn't even remember. But being here in the presence of nature, of finally giving into my instincts and letting myself be free...I couldn't even begin to describe it.

It felt right. It felt like this was where I was supposed to be. This was what I was supposed to be doing, all this time.

My dragon no longer stayed locked away inside my heart. I was the dragon, and the dragon was me.

And it was time to fly.

I pushed off of the ground with my strong back legs, stretching my wings wide to catch the air. I knew what to do on instinct, even though it had been so long. I leapt forward and caught the air current, tucking my legs beneath me as I sailed into the sky.

The ground fell away, growing smaller and smaller as I ascended. The air up here was even cooler, thick with frost and clouds, but it didn't matter. The fire in my blood ran through me, keeping away every chill. I was soaring, floating, dancing through the air on wings as wide as a house. The Valley stretched out below me, every building and feature dollhouse sized at this height. I swept my gaze from the gazebo in the town square to the rotunda of the Town Hall where I'd met Rosemary over the colorful tents of the market and up the path to the cabins...

To the Dozing Dragon.

There it stood, proud against the ivory backdrop of the

Valley. I could see each eave from up here. Each slope of the roof. Each window. This old house had been in our family for generations. It was a cornerstone of culture, life, and laughter for each citizen, no matter how different.

And now, there was an omega in that bed and breakfast. An omega who was waiting for me. My mate.

I flapped my wings harder, gaining yet more altitude. I sailed toward the hill where the bed and breakfast lay, high enough up to not be seen.

There was something different about seeing things from above. Something about a new perspective that changed everything.

Up here, there was nothing to cloud my mind. Up here, there were no distractions of everyday life. Living as a shifter was freeing, in some ways, but it meant you could never run from your demons. And they were here in full force today, sneaking out of their hiding places and hitting me with as much force as the wind.

Emotions and memories came at me one after another. Perhaps it had to do with connecting with my dragon form after so long. Perhaps I had just not allowed myself to come to terms with my mom's death. Perhaps it was finally time to grieve.

I weakened and dropped altitude, thinking only of her smile, her laugh, her hugs. If I could have seen her just one more time...could have told her, could have fixed things...

But she was gone. Never to return.

How do you come back from that?

Dragons don't have funerals like humans do. Instead of burying their dead, dragons cremate them. It's a fitting way to go, "returning to the flames" as they call it. And my mother's cremation was scheduled for the next day. I'd nearly forgotten with everything else going on, but now it came back to me at full force.

Tomorrow, I'd watch the flames devour my mother and spread her ashes to the wind.

I just hoped I could make her proud.

I drooped downward further, coming in for a landing in the same meadow I'd played all those years.

It was fitting, to return here upon her death. Perhaps we could even hold the cremation ceremony here. She'd like that.

"For you, mom," I whispered, kneeling in the snow. Sparks crackled on my tongue and this time I wasn't afraid. They ignited and flared out in one long, hot breath, melting the snow instantly and singing the ground. My face grew hot, and I wasn't sure if the drops of moisture on my face were sweat or tears. I kept breathing, kept howling, marking a place on the ground that would be forever hers.

A small, black spiral, with an arrow at each end. It was the same symbol Nellie had worn around her neck all these years. And she would return to the flames with it as well.

"All things are circular," she would tell me. "We give and take constantly, but in the end all things return to the universe."

I stopped finally, out of breath and out of time. My shoulders sagged and shook. This time I didn't try to stop it. I gazed upon the spiral burnt into the earth, and I sobbed.

BEHIND CLOSED DOORS

WILL

*A*mazing what a good nap can do for you. I woke feeling refreshed, if a little disoriented. Then my hand went to my stomach.

Oh right. That.

I threw my legs over the side of the bed, grateful that the nausea had passed. Besides the nagging anxiety about whether I was pregnant, I felt good as new. Nellie always kept the beds here in top form, expertly fluffed. After sleeping in one, I saw now what the fuss was all about.

It was more than a bed. It was like, an experience. Which sounds totally cheesy to say, but have you ever woken up from the best nap of your life, feeling like you could take on the world and then some?

Yeah, it was like that.

After a quick trip to the bathroom to freshen up, I peeked around the inn for Sebastian. Couldn't find him, so I figured he was still meeting with Rosemary. I checked my watch.

I'd slept for a good two hours. He'd probably be back soon, but in the meantime, I had an idea.

While I slept, I dreamed about the old Festival of Fire. I saw the colors, the smells of roasting chestnuts, the music in the background as the lights flickered on and off in rhythm. It was more than just a simple tree lighting ceremony or something like that. It was a performance. Held each Saturday in December, it had been one of the town's biggest spectacles.

Had, being the operative word.

But not for much longer, if I had anything to do with it.

Sebastian was right. The Festival had been wonderful, and the tragedy of years past couldn't stop us from spreading joy and laughter this year. Besides, I thought with a sad smile, it's what Miss Walker would have wanted.

I was going to bring back the Festival of Fire. If that

didn't convince Sebastian to stick around, nothing would.

Not many people knew where the supplies for the Festival were kept. I only did because I was living with the lady that ran the show at the time. Ever since the fire, the sparklers and matches and rockets had stayed locked away in a storage unit, gathering dust. But I knew just where to find them.

I lived in Miss Walker's old house, after all. When she passed away, it only seemed fitting for me to keep the cabin. It wasn't much to look at, but it was home. As home as I'd ever been.

I picked up the pace, grabbing my coat by the door before slipping out of the Bed and Breakfast and down the road toward town. If I was quick enough, Sebastian would never even notice I was gone.

Sebastian.

Another wave of emotion hit me then. Or was that nausea?

We'd grown so close in so little time. I wanted to trust

him more than anything, but if he tried to double cross me...

I gritted my teeth. No. He wouldn't. He wasn't Brad.

I just hoped that my fear didn't tank our relationship before it begun.

The walk across town was easy enough. Not many people out on the roads today, only a few neighbors walking their dogs or children playing in the snow. I saw Ren Svenson, owner of the creperie, talking to someone at a market stall and gave him a wave.

That was the thing about small towns like this. Everyone knew everyone. That was both a pro, and a con.

Not easy keeping secrets around here, and if I was gonna pull this off, I'd need discretion.

Finally I reached my place on the other side of town. It was far from the town center, only flanked by a few sparse cabins. Miss Walker liked her privacy just as much as I liked mine. Maybe that's why we got along so well.

Instead of entering the house, I circled around and unlocked the gate that led to the back yard. The gate creaked and whined, frozen and stuck in a snow drift.

With a grunt and a push, I yanked it free. Not before spraying myself with slush, though.

I shook myself off and tried to forget the chill. Was it just me, or was it getting colder by the second? I pushed that thought away and clomped through the freshly fallen snow to the shed in the backyard.

The ancient bolt was still there, untouched. I dug out my key ring again and froze. Wait a second. This wasn't the lock I remembered.

The key I owned was small and light, for an equally dainty lock. But the padlock sealing the shed now was sturdy, thick steel with a complicated-looking keyhole. I furrowed my brow and shuffled through my keys. Nothing looked like it would fit.

Since when had she changed the lock? Had that happened without me knowing?

No one had been back here since she died in the accident. She always took the liberty of retrieving and re-packing all the years supplies herself, carting them to and from the square each year.

So clearly, she must have changed the lock. Must have been right before she died.

And now? Where, or what, the key was was anyone's guess.

I let out a sigh. Then with a groan I grabbed the frosty door handle and pulled, hard. No luck.

If I couldn't get into the shed, we couldn't have the Festival of Fire.

And I could just imagine the hurt on Sebastian's face all over again. No. I needed to do this. I'd figure out a way. Vale Valley was getting fireworks, dammit.

Will Sterling didn't give up that easily.

DOZING NO MORE

SEBASTIAN

I needed to see him.

Needed him more than I needed air. The flight had cleared my head just like Rose said it would. Up there in the clouds, I could see what my real priorities were. And they just so happened to include my omega mate.

I rushed back toward the bed and breakfast, hoping that Will was feeling better. I'd hated to leave him looking so sick like that. I knew I was probably being over cautious but we were so new, so freshly mated. If anything happened to him, I didn't know what I would do.

The hill fell away as I took the steps two at a time, even breaking a light sweat in the chilly air. When I wrenched open the front door and made a beeline for wills room, I had a gnawing, sickening feeling in the pit of my stomach.

Nerves. Just nerves.

But when I threw open the door and found only an empty bed, I knew it was more than that.

"Will?" I called through the house. My voice echoed through the long twisty hallways and came back to me. "Will? You in here?" I peered in the nearby rooms. The kitchen. The bathroom. Nothing.

Maybe we'd just passed one another. Or, I told myself, finally he decided to go back to his place. He hadn't really packed any clothes or supplies for over here, after all. He must have been wanting some clean clothes and a shower. There was nothing to worry about.

Except I worried about everything anyway. My mate was out there, and I needed to talk to him. I needed to make sure he knew how I felt, before it was too late.

I stopped dead in my tracks when I saw Will's sparkling scarf still hanging on the rack near the door. Why would he have left that, unless he was in a great hurry? He'd seemed to like it so much.

I tilted my head, considering the warm, soft stitches. It reminded me of him already. His smiles, his warmth, his thin, sprightly body spread out beside mine. Even his faint, spicy cinnamon scent.

And here I thought that returning to Vale Valley would be depressing. I'd thought it would be a quick in and out kind of trip, but now I wasn't quite sure of anything anymore. Did everyone go this crazy over their mates?

Cause I sure felt like I was losing it over mine.

The phone rang in my pocket again, shaking me out of my thoughts. What the hell? That was the third time today! I'd told everyone at the office not to bother me, and I had no idea who else it could be, but if they kept calling...

I sighed, sat down, and answered the call.

"Hello?"

"Dude, where the hell have you been?" The impatient voice crowed at me instantly and I jerked the phone away from my ear.

"Whoa, whoa, calm down. What's going on?" I still held the phone at arm's length. Getting shouted at was the last thing I needed today.

"I've been trying to get in touch with you forever."

"And?" Spit it out already.

"There's been a...change." He spoke the next words carefully, delicately. "The deal that you signed off on, before you left. It...ah, didn't go through."

I sat bolt upright, eyes wide. "What?"

"The other party turned us down at the last minute. And I mean the last minute, man. We were all set, due diligence done, everything. We'd spoken to their lawyers and were assured it was airtight, but then..." I could almost hear the helpless shrug over the phone. "I dunno, man."

I scraped a hand down my face and through my hair. That deal was supposed to be our big break. Without it, we would be...

"So you know that this means."

I squeezed my eyes shut, praying there was another solution. Another way.

"I know you said not to bother you while you were on your trip, but we were really counting on that capital." He paused for a moment. Sighed. "I need your authorization to seek out bridge funding."

I winced again. "So soon? I thought we had plenty of runway left."

"Remember those holiday bonuses?" He reminded me.

"Maybe not such a good idea after all. And we can't exactly ask people to un spend their Christmas money."

"Fuck," I breathed, leaning back in the chair. I stared at the ceiling and tried to think of some way out of this. How had we fallen so far, so quickly? I mean, I knew we were playing a high risk high reward game, but everything seemed so certain. So stable. And then this. Losing our biggest client meant we were gonna be hard up for cash, and soon.

"What should I tell the team, sir?" His voice remained cool, businesslike, but I knew this situation was anything but. I wanted to be a good manager. A good business owner. I wanted to make my people happy, and built something together. Now all of that looked to be in jeopardy, and it was all my fault.

"I..." I stammered, sighing. "I don't know. Buy me some time. I'll think of something."

A pause hung on the line, the tension thickening.

"Hope you're well," the man said finally, his words clipped. "And my condolences about your mother."

"Thanks," I mumbled, but my brain was already elsewhere.

"I'll call you back soon," I promised. "Don't do anything

drastic." With that, I pressed the 'end call' button and buried my face in my hands.

I GUESS I REALLY COULDN'T HAVE MY CAKE AND EAT it too. The more I thought about things, the more the two paths diverged in front of me. I could go back to New York, damage control, save the day. But in doing so, I'd have to leave Will. I wasn't under any delusions that he'd want to come up to the city with me, even if we were mates. He was a soft, gentle soul that much preferred peace and privacy. As much as I wanted him around, I knew the fast paced life of NYC would only stifle him.

And the other option? I wasn't sure I was ready to do that either. So here I was, once again stuck at an impasse. Only this time, it wasn't a difficult logic puzzle or a hypothetical business school case study.

It was real life, and the decision I made here would have a very real impact on not just my future, but my team's. And my mate's.

I stared at Nellie's will, laying on the coffee table next to the armchairs and the fireplace. I remembered Rosemary's words. Her ultimatum.

It wasn't too late. I could still give up the Dozing Dragon. Put it on the market. Sell the place.

It would give me the influx of cash we needed, and I wouldn't have to break the bad news to the team. It was almost a perfect plan.

A perfect plan for old Sebastian, anyway.

For this new guy? Hell, I didn't even know.

I paced back and forth in the living room, chewing my lip and trying to think.

To sell, or not to sell?

To stay, or to go?

Will's scarf warmed in my hands. I glared at it and back to the fireplace. Had it gotten too close and caught fire? No, that wasn't right. There was something happening to it.

Love in every stitch, I remembered the sign at the market stall. I'd thought the man was just talking up his creations at the time, but this was Vale Valley, after all. Was there a chance that it could actually be magic?

It will always help you find your way home, he'd told Will with serious eyes.

Did it help if even I didn't know where my true home was? I was torn between two worlds. Two lives.

So I did what Rosemary had been telling me to do all this time.

I took a deep breath, let it out, and let go. All of my worries and fears went into that scarf, all of my love and concern and care. I hoped, no, prayed with every fiber of my being that I would make the right choice. And that it would show me the way.

The fibers began to glow, casting a warm yellow light around me. I watched it, unbelieving, as the thing began to move.

It's working, I thought breathlessly. *It's actually working!*

I wrapped the scarf around my neck and opened the door, taking the first step toward my destiny.

THE MISSING KEY

WILL

I paced around the kitchen, trying to come up with a plan.

So the shed was locked. Fine. I could break the lock somehow, or pick it, or find the key. I could even try and recreate it, gather up all the supplies anew. But that required time and money I didn't have. Which left the shed.

"Now would be a good time for a little ghostly assistance," I said to the empty room. No one came. Of course not. They were always barging in my business when I was trying to do something else, but now that I actually needed help? Nowhere to be found. Typical.

I sighed and walked back out into the living room,

sinking down onto the couch. My stomach cramped again, bringing up that uneasy fear once more.

Right. I needed to figure that out, too. And time was running out.

Nellie's cremation ceremony was tomorrow, and after that? There would be nothing holding him here. He could move on with his life.

But what if he knew I was with child? Would that be enough to convince him to stay?

I groaned. That sounded so...manipulative. It's not like I got pregnant on purpose just to pull him away from his life in New York!

But I also knew that if I ever tried to live there, I'd probably go crazy. I lived in a small town, hell, on the outskirts of a small town, for a reason. I was acquainted with enough spirits passing by in just the Valley. I couldn't imagine the overwhelming tides of them in a city as big as New York.

As much as I wanted to, that would be no place for an omega like me.

Or for our child.

Why did this have to be so complicated? I covered my face with a pillow and screamed, letting out my frustration, anger, and fear. I beat the cushion, wailed, kicked, screamed.

Did it change things? Not in the slightest. But I felt a little better afterward, if even more tired than before.

There was only one thing to do. I needed to start searching for the key.

AN HOUR PASSED AND I STILL HAD NOTHING TO show for it. My knees ached from crawling around looking under counters and furniture, and my stomach rumbled with hunger. So much for my heroic efforts. Any minute now, Seb would return to the Dozing Dragon and find me gone. Would he come looking for me? Would he even like what he found?

I stood up too quickly and lost my balance. I swayed to one side and gripped the side of the couch, but my knees still buckled. I fell down on the couch, my mind spinning, my vision blurring. Everything went black for a fraction of a second, and then...I saw her.

"Hello?" A small voice came from behind me. I knew that voice. Hadn't heard it since...

"Miss Walker?" I said, the words feeling like mush in my mouth. "Is that you?"

"Quiet, child. Listen to me."

I swallowed. Was I just hallucinating after my fall? Or had I finally found her?

"Where are you?" I called out again, righting myself. I was still dizzy, but the worst of it had passed. My limbs felt like jello, though, and I wasn't sure I'd be able to make it far.

I whirled around but the source of the sound changed. It seemed to follow me, almost as if she was speaking to me from inside my mind. "I can't see you," I said, still peering into the empty room. Was I looking for something that didn't exist?

"That's all right, darling. I'm up here." I felt a small tap on the side of my skull and yelped, clasping at my head.

"You're in my brain?!" I cried, clawing at my hair.

"Relax, Will! Nothing so gruesome as that. You know I never liked company. I'm just...well, not able to show myself just yet. I've been hiding, you see. But I've been watching you, even from beyond."

My heart hitched at those words. She'd taken such good care of me when I came to Vale Valley seeking refuge.

She'd listened to me and believed in me at a time when no one else did. Losing her was one of the hardest things I'd ever gone through.

But she was still here? Watching?

"Yes, I know about your gifts, Will. And I know how much they scare you, too."

"I—" I started, already on the defensive. But it was no use. She saw right through me. Maybe I was the transparent one.

Ever since I was young, seeing the spirits of dead people had been a disability. Not something to be proud of. Something to be shunned, hidden, ignored, at best. Even with all the magic and diversity of Vale Valley surrounding me, I still felt like an outcast.

I'd never fully accepted my powers or tried to use them for good. I mostly tried to get them to go away.

What if I could actually help, though? What if my ability helped me save the bed and breakfast, the town, and the relationship all in one fell swoop?

I had to try.

I let out a long, cleansing breath. I released my fear and anger. I opened my eyes, and there she was.

Miss Walker.

She looked just like I'd remembered her. Old, yes, but the kind of sweet old lady that's a mother to everyone. She beamed down at me with pride in her eyes.

"You can see me now, Will. You always could, really. But you had to allow yourself to lean into it."

Seeing her there in front of me, I was suddenly at a loss for words. I had so many things I wanted to say to her. So many things I wanted to thank her for, or ask her...

Vale Valley just hadn't been the same since she passed away.

"I think its time we bring a little spark back to the Valley, don't you think?" Her eyes gleamed with that familiar excitement. "I saw you wrestling with my shed."

"Do you know where the key is?" I asked. "The one I have didn't work."

"Ah," she said, a small frown crossing her face. "You know, I'd forgotten I'd replaced the lock on that thing too. It all happened so fast when, you know..." she twirled her hand in a vague gesture. "I wish I could have been there for you longer."

I blinked, my eyes wet. A single tear spilled over and down my cheek. She'd been like a mother to me.

"Tell me, though." She glided to the other side of the couch and rested her chin on her hands. "What made you so eager to get into them now? It's been five years, Will."

I winced. It didn't feel like that long. Seemed like only yesterday I watched in horror as the firecrackers exploded on the ground, sending debris and fire everywhere. And the screams...

So why had I had a change of heart? I knew the answer instantly. Those warm brown eyes. That maddening smile. The strong arms that wrapped around me so protectively, the ones I never wanted to let go.

"My mate," I said at last. I liked the way it felt on my tongue. "I'm...I found my mate, Miss Walker. And he loves the fireworks. Loves them. He has just returned to town after so long, and was really hoping to see them, and..." I trailed off, out of breath.

She slid down beside me, sinking into the floor so that she could look up into my downturned face. Damn creepy, but endearing all the same.

"I had hoped it was something like that, sweetheart. I can see it from the look in your eyes. You're smitten."

I huffed out a nervous laugh and looked away. No getting away from a ghost stare, though.

"Yeah," I breathed finally. My hand went up to caress the still tender spot where Sebastian had claimed me. "I guess I am."

"And that's what the season is all about, isn't it? Spending time with the ones you love."

At her words, something swelled inside me. Something bigger than myself. Even my stomach got in on it, clenching and unclenching in some weird sort of joy.

"I'll tell you where the key is. You've earned it. Now go on. Bring the Festival of Fire back to Vale Valley. Go get your man."

I COULDN'T BELIEVE IT. KEY IN HAND, I RUSHED FOR the shed, my mind still reeling from the ghostly encounter. I'd actually done it. I'd actually controlled my powers for once. And if this worked, well...it could change everything.

My hand shook as I slipped the key into the lock. I held my breath and turned it.

Click.

The lock swung open.

I quickly removed it and stuffed it into my pocket, then stood back as the sturdy doors swung open.

It smelled. That much was a given. It had been locked up for years with no ventilation. I just hoped that the fireworks were still all right and hadn't gotten too damp.

I peered into the darkness of the shed and brushed aside a cobweb. My phone acted as a flashlight, and it all came back to me.

The piles of firecrackers. The rockets. The small little jets that squealed and showered sparks all over. And my favorite: the sparklers. They acted like little magic wands, spraying colors and sparks whereever you waved it. Miss Walker used to pass them out to all the kids and light them. When it was dark, you could wave it around and write your name in fire. It was a simple pleasure, but one of my most vivid memories of the old days.

The shed had sealed well. Despite the rains and snows the materials within remained dry. Besides being a little musty smelling, they would be good to go. Now I just had to get Rosemary's blessing, rouse the townsfolk, and get these down to the square before dark.

This would be a night to remember.

I NEARLY RAN INTO ROSEMARY AS I CAUGHT HER leaving Town Hall. She lunged out of the way just in time, and a good thing too, because I was sprinting with such momentum I ran into the now closed door of the Town Hall, jarring my bones.

"What's got you in such a rush?" She asked, laughing. "You just about bowled me over!"

"Rosemary," I gasped, catching my breath. "The Festival of Fire...I figured it out...the shed..."

"Slow down, Will. Do you need a drink? I was just on my way out but I can go in and fix you a cup of tea if you like?"

"I'm fine. Sorry. Just wanted to come down here as soon as I could. Have you seen Sebastian today?"

A flash of recognition. "I did. He was just here a few hours ago. You looking for him?"

"I've got an idea. Something special for him. Can we go in and talk?"

"Well," Rosemary said, wrapping her shawl around her. "I was just about to go run some errands, but I can tell you've got something big to tell me. It can wait. Come on."

She turned and opened the door, and I followed her in.

"I always knew you and Sebastian would make a good match," she mused before I even got sat down. I stared at her agape, but she simply shrugged.

"Come on, it's obvious. He comes down here asking for advice, then you show up looking all flustered. Adorable, really."

"Do you know where he went?"

Rose tilted her head. "Out."

"He's..." I started, almost afraid to finish the sentence. "He's coming back, right?"

I didn't know what I would do if he didn't.

"Oh, I think so. He just needed some time to think, is all. He'll be back, though. I can feel it." She hung up her shawl and moved toward the kitchen, calling over her shoulder. "Tea?"

I followed her, not willing to waste time. I was just about to protest again when my stomach grumbled.

"Maybe you have some snacks instead?" I asked hopefully.

"Hmm...I just sent Sebastian away with the last of the cookies, but I'm sure I can dig up something."

While she was rummaging through the cabinets in the small kitchen, I reached into my pocket and held out the key.

"Rosemary. You remember the Festival of Fire."

"I do," she said, still peering into the pantry. "Real shame what happened, too."

"What if I told you I found the key to the shed? That I wanna bring it back again? For Seb?"

This time, she did turn around. Her whole face lit up. "I think that's a wonderful idea. What do you need from me?"

"Your blessing," I stated. "And some helping hands to bring down the supplies from the shed. Think you know some people who can help?"

"You're thinking of doing it tonight?" She asked. "Such short notice."

"No time like the present, right? And I figure, Sebastian might not be here for much longer, and..." I trailed off again. Didn't want to think of that.

Rosemary considered that for a moment. Then she

placed a hand on my shoulder, her eyes far away. Finally, she nodded, as if snapping out of a trance. Without another word, she turned on her heel and went back to the coat rack, bundling up all over again.

"So you'll help me?" I jogged to catch up with her.

She turned and grinned, wrapping the shawl tight around her shoulders. Excitement flowed off of her like a child on Christmas. If her smile got any larger I thought she might break. "I've been waiting for a moment like this for years. Let's go, we can round up some helpers on the way."

And with that, we hurried out the door and up toward my house, where the fireworks were waiting.

After all, the show must go on.

A NIGHT TO REMEMBER

SEBASTIAN

*H*ard to say how I knew exactly where to go. Be it magic, intuition, or fate, my feet moved before I consciously knew where we were going. The whole time, my heart pattered out a frantic rhythm, my dragon coiling and crying out. He'd made his intentions clear, at least.

"Mate! Mate! Mine! Mine!"

I weaved through the forest, taking a roughshod path through the sticks and leaves. It didn't matter that I wasn't on the road. I was simply following the scarf, and trusting that it would know where to go.

All the while, something built within me. A rising tide of emotion daring to reach a crescendo. I couldn't quite place my finger on it, but something had...changed about the connection between Will and I. I felt him more closely, more keenly than I ever had before, and I knew I'd be able to find him, even if the scarf couldn't.

Next, I had to plan what I was going to say. I still didn't know what to choose. Will and Vale Valley or New York and business? Was there perhaps a way to have both?

I remembered again Hannah's face lighting up with laughter. Her jingle bell pigtails. The look in her eyes when she talked about the spirit of Christmas.

Finally, after all this time, I think I realized what she was talking about.

I'd spent so much time working, striving, perfecting, that I'd totally neglected my true nature. Outside the Valley walls I was able to distract myself and ignore it, but here among my brethren it came out of me more strongly than ever before. In suppressing my nature I'd not only become jaded and lonely, but had forgotten what it meant to say hi to a neighbor or help a loved one in need.

Even though this trip was unexpected, perhaps it was just what I needed after all.

Boom!

I startled and looked up, the explosion catching me off

guard. There, in the sunset-splattered sky, was a shower of red and gold sparks, twinkling and falling lazily toward the ground.

I blinked, waited. Then came another, louder boom. Blue this time, lighting up the sky for that precious instant and sparkling, raining, down to the earth.

Fireworks.

Oh my god. Fireworks!

I rushed toward the sound, nearly shifting into dragon form in my excitement. The Festival! It screeched inside me. Now not only the scarf was pulling me forward. It was every fiber of my being, reaching out and pulling me where I needed to be.

Will had told me the Festival of Fire had ended five years ago. That they couldn't hold it anymore, after an accident. But when I heard another shattering explosion and watched the colors twinkle against the twilight, I hoped against hope that he was wrong.

I pushed through the remaining line of trees and came out onto a clearing.

I knew this place.

And I knew these people.

I watched, wild eyed and delirious, as Will's face broke into an ecstatic grin and he lowered a match, waving to me.

Rosemary Vale was there. My old friends were there. Everyone I knew and cared for in the Valley had pitched in, it seemed. And as another firecracker exploded above us, I knew that the scarf and my heart were leading me to the same place.

Home.

My real home.

I ran forward and threw my arms around Will's neck, picking him up and spinning him around. He let out the most adorable little squeak, clinging to me as the world slowed to a crawl.

"You didn't," I breathed, looking at the display around us.

Will's eyes were large, shiny with excitement. "You said it was your favorite."

I couldn't believe it. I laughed, shook my head. Brought him closer. "You did all this for me?"

"It's not a Vale Valley Christmas without you," he mumbled.

I didn't need any more convincing. I took his face in my hands, tilting his chin upward, and kissed him.

Cheers erupted from the crowd around us. Applause too. But it seemed so far away when my mate was next to me. Nothing else in the world mattered when I had him in my arms. How could I have been so foolish not to see what was right in front of me?

"You're really something, you know that?" I rested my forehead against his, our eyes still locked. Within them danced his concern, his happiness, and yes...his love.

"So it worked?" Will choked. "I don't want to lose you."

My dragon cried out in pain just at the thought. No. I could never leave him. I knew that now.

I ran a hand through his hair, brushed it away from his ear, and whispered. "Never again, my little one. Never again."

I kissed him again, this time faster, hotter, fiercer. And you know how people say that their kiss felt like fireworks? Well, this time it really was. Explosions and cheers went up around us, and as I claimed my mate's lips, two twin rockets sailed toward the sky, twining around and around each other like two halves of a whole.

I looked up just in time to see the climax, an earth-shaking boom where the two points of light collided. They exploded into a giant heart shape of green and white each spark a delicious reminder of our bond.

He was mine, and I was his.

The way it should be.

"I'm glad you came back," Will whispered, pecking a kiss along my jaw.

I held up the scarf I'd bought for him, shaking the tassels. I shrugged. "I had a little help...guess it really does help you find home after all."

Will's face lit up in a smile so bright it could banish the deepest darkness. And there, in the pits of my heart and soul, the last barrier came down. My dragon took control of my senses and I purred a deep, satisfying growl.

We were one and the same now. I was no longer afraid.

NELLIE'S SECRET

SEBASTIAN

The day had come at last. I'd been so busy with everything else that cropped up once I arrived in Diamond Falls—The Dozing Dragon, the Market, the Festival, not to mention my adorable mate— that when the day came it felt like a surprise. Even though that was the whole reason I'd come to the Valley in the first place.

It was time for my mother's cremation.

As dragons, we didn't believe in burying our dead. Sounded far too claustrophobic, if you asked me. So instead we held an elaborate cremation ritual to return our souls to the air and the flames. This way, we'd always be aloft in the winds, sailing through the world and watching over our loved ones from above.

The funeral pyre had been built. The casket had been prepared. The only thing left was the burning ritual.

My hands shook as I tried to button up my shirt. Tradition said that the next of kin would light the first flame. But she was my mother, not a piece of kindling. Even though i knew it would set her into the next plane and the next life, I had a hard time wrapping my mind around it.

You're going to set fire to your mother. You're going to watch her burn.

"You doing okay?" Will asked, coming up behind me. He slipped his thin arms around my waist and squeezed. "You look nervous."

"Wouldn't you be?" I turned to him. "How do I look?"

"You're one button off," he pointed. "Let me."

"You don't have to—" I started to protest, but my omega was too quick. He expertly undid each button from top to bottom, placing kisses against my bare chest at each interval. Well, when this was included, I wasn't complaining...

"Mmm," I growled deep in my chest, weaving my fingers through his hair. "You know just how to get me."

"And you're totally distracted from being nervous now, right?"

I glared at him.

"So it worked."

Shaking my head, I barked out a laugh. "I guess it did." Then I gave him a quick kiss on the cheek. "Go get ready. They're expecting us soon."

As my omega left the room, I couldn't help but watch the sway of his hips or the curve of his ass. What had I ever done to deserve such a perfect mate?

WITH MY SHIRT PROPERLY BUTTONED THIS TIME, I led Will toward the clearing where we'd perform the ceremony. Snow fell gently, but the wind had let up, at least. Will wore his infamous purple scarf and gloves, while I'd put on my heaviest woolen coat. Not that I'd need it for long.

We didn't see many people as we passed. Perhaps they were already at the ceremony, or perhaps they were simply indoors, enjoying the hearth and a warm meal. Wish I could be, right now.

But we had something even more important to attend to.

"Remember to breathe," Will reminded me with a squeeze of my hand. "You can do this."

"Sure you can't like, talk to her or something?" I shrugged. Will was the only person I knew who had the power to speak to spirits, and even he didn't understand it that well.

Will shook his head. "I've tried. She's a tricky one."

"I know. I just...wish I could have talked to her again, you know?"

"Yeah," Will agreed. Then, changing the subject, he said, "I've never seen this ritual before. Not many dragons around these parts."

"I only vaguely remember it, myself. But it would be doing Nellie a disservice if we didn't do it for her. She's a dragon, just like I am. The same magical blood runs through our veins, and when our time comes to an end, we must be released back into the flames."

Will mused on that for a few moments, the only sounds the crunching of our boots in the snow. "It's rather poetic, isn't it?"

"Huh?" I raised an eyebrow, caught off guard by the sudden question.

"You're a dragon, made of fire. And when you die...you

burn. Letting the fire reclaim your body and reform it into something new. Sounds a lot cooler than rotting underground." He shrugged. "Do you have any other traditions like that?"

I knew he was trying to keep my mind off the task at hand. But I didn't mind talking. And were it any other time, I would have launched into a whole explanation of every old legend I knew. But the clearing drew close, and with it the smell of fresh wood.

Villagers had already begun the preparations.

There weren't many people gathered in the clearing when we arrived, but I liked it that way. Something told me Nellie would have, as well. She was a kind, gentle soul, ready to open up her home to anyone who needed it, but behind closed doors she became a very private person. That was a side many didn't see of her. I did.

So it was fitting that only a few of us were here to mourn her passing and celebrate her life. Her most trusted friends and neighbors. Everyone who she would have wanted by her side at the end.

As soon as I lay eyes on the casket, my heart clenched in my chest. I wasn't ready for this. I couldn't.

But Will stood beside me, never wavering, giving me

strength. If it wasn't for him, I didn't think I could have gone through with it at all.

We passed over the spot where I'd carved the burnt spiral into the earth and my dragon did a little loop de loop in my chest. Soon, this whole place would burn. And Nellie with it.

We reached the center of the clearing, the exact point where the fullest moon of the season would reach its zenith and smile upon us.

"Greetings, friends of Vale Valley." I called out to the crowd, projecting my voice as strongly as I could. "Thank you all for coming out here today. It is this night that we honor the life of Nellie Nicole Wallace, and remember the great blessings she has bestowed upon this town."

A murmur passed through the crowd.

"If you would like to say a piece about Nellie, now is your time. Trust that your words will reach up into the heavens this night, and carry with her to the next plane."

Rosemary came forward. She placed a heap of sage on top of the casket, lowering her head. "Nellie was such a bright light in this town. She saw the best in everyone, and always had a room for anyone in need."

Nods and rumbles of agreement.

"And her culinary expertise…" another man came forward with a bunch of flowers. I couldn't remember his name, but I'd seen him in the flower shop a couple of times. He collected succulents. "Her beef stew was to die for." He winced at the unfortunate word. "Uh, sorry."

Will stepped forward next, leaving my side to peer over the casket. It was already heaped with herbs and flowers and mementos. All the things that she'd want to bring with her in the next life.

I squeezed my eyes shut, willing the tears to go away. All these people had such great memories of her. All these people had been there for her when I had not.

If only I could go back and change things…

"I didn't know Nellie very well," Will said in a wavery voice. "Not personally, anyway. But she was one of my best customers, and always wanted her place to be filled with light and life. Anyone that knew her could feel the love and compassion radiating off of her like a sun. She brought it to every room, every gathering. And Vale Valley is darker today without her."

"Hear hear," someone agreed, dabbing at their face.

And so it went. Neighbor after neighbor approached to pay their respects, sharing their anecdotes and memories. Some of them were funny. Some of them were sad. But they were all real, raw stories of the town and the people she made an impact on, every day. I I did my best to stand there and look the part of the dutiful alpha son, but with each story, another memory of my own leapt onto the pile. She had given so much, meant so much to so many people. I saw that now, and I sagged under the weight of it all.

Will returned to my side and took my hand, leading me to the small altar on top of the funeral pyre. My mother's casket lay there, embellished with so many trinkets and flowers it was barely visible. I placed a hand on the smooth wood, feeling the last of her energy. I remembered her smile. Her laugh. Even that stern look she gave me when I knew I'd done something wrong.

"From this plane, to the next. We will meet again," I whispered. Then I reached low, all the way to my core, calling up my dragon spirit. It was easier this time to catch and tame the flames. They wrapped around me and through me until we were one, then I let out a final breath, fire lighting the night sky and catching on the dry brush around her.

"Goodbye," I said, and stepped down from the platform.

The flames flickered and caught, crawling from the dry weeds and brush up to the planks of the casket and around it. We stood there, holding hands and mourning the life that had been. The pyre sparked, crackled, and flared toward the sky. In time it became a raging inferno. A testament to all the light she'd provided us in life.

WE SAT THERE FOR GOD KNOWS HOW LONG, LETTING the heat of the fire warm us and keep us company on this cold winter's night. My eyes danced with visions of flames and all the memories of the past. My heart hurt for her, knowing that she was leaving us, but it was glad, as well. She'd always loved flying. And now she'd get to do that forever, carried on the winds of fate.

"You ready?" Will asked me after a long while. Almost everyone had left except for us, and the flames were starting to burn lower now. No longer the raging inferno it once was, the flames crackled at the edges of the ruined pyre like feathers, gentle and trembling. Ash rained from the sky and lifted in the winds, swirling through the air. There she goes, I thought. On to the next great adventure.

I got up and stretched my legs, my stiff joints making some awful popping sounds as I did so. I rubbed my hands together and stuffed them in my pockets. If I was getting cold, then poor Will must be freezing!

"Let's go home," I said, pulling him to me. I planted a kiss on his forehead and buried my face in his scarf for a moment. Good excuse to wipe away the cold tears streaking my face.

"Home?" Will repeated. "And where's that?" His eyes shone, forever hopeful. How could I say no to that? The scarf, and Nellie, and all of Vale Valley screamed at me to stay. And this time, all I had to do was listen.

"Right here with you," I said, and kissed him.

IT WAS NEARLY DAWN WHEN WE GOT BACK TO THE Dozing Dragon. I'd offered to drop Will off at his place, but he wouldn't hear of it.

"I want to stay with you," he'd said, never leaving my side.

And he didn't know just how much that meant to me.

I was putting my coat away on the rack when I heard a yelp from the den. "Sebastian!" Will screamed. Sounded terrified.

I nearly knocked the coat rack over in my haste, rushing down the hall and toward the sound. When I stopped in front of the fireplace, my mouth dropped open as well.

The heart was just as I had left it. Well, almost. Instead of a normal, orange-red flame in the fireplace, the fire was green, and the flames licked higher than any I'd ever seen before.

"Can you see that?" Will asked, pointing a shaking finger at the fireplace. I squinted, unsure if he was talking about the green flames or something else.

"What do you see?" I asked, still staring. The flames changed again, this time sliding into the blue spectrum. They danced and twisted like they had a mind of their own, curling and shaping until...a face formed.

Nellie's face.

"Stones and scales!" I yelped, backpedaling. I'd seen her burn! Seen it!

But there was no mistaking those all-knowing eyes. The slope of her nose. The strands of hair hanging into her face, even through the lick of the flames.

"N-Nellie?" I gasped, my voice failing.

The color changed again, becoming a deep fuchsia this time. "Sebastian."

The voice came from everywhere all at once, and nowhere. Felt like she was speaking from within me.

I blinked and swallowed, taking a tentative step forward.

"Am I...am I seeing things right now? You see her too Will, right?" I gripped the side of the couch for support, feeling the rough texture of the fabric on the pads of my fingertips. Yes. This was real. I was here. And I was seeing my dead mother in the flames. Vale Valley wasn't done surprising me yet.

"Yeah," Will said, looking almost as surprised as I did. "But I've never seen a spirit manifest in this way before."

"You sent me to the flames and the air," the spirit said simply. The fire crackled in an upward burst and the apparition did a sort of spin. "That is our way."

It was. But this?

"I had to come back and see you, honey. One last time. Not gonna say it was easy, though."

"Are you...are you okay?" I asked, taking another step forward. "Mom..."

Fire-Nellie shrugged and gave me that 'what do you think?' kind of grin I remembered so well. "Besides the matter of being dead, yeah, I'd say I am. I can't linger here for long, but there's something I wanted to tell you." She paused and looked between us. "Both of you."

I glanced at Will.

"What is it?"

"I've lived a full, happy life. I'm just glad I got to see your face one more time." She blinked, and even through the flickery apparition I could see what looked like tears.

"Mom, I'm so sorry," I started. My voice was raw, my chest seizing with emotion. "I should have come back. I should have checked on you. I—"

"You had to find your path, Sebbie. We all do."

I huffed out a breath that turned into a smile. Sebbie. Her old nickname for me. I'd thought it was so cringe back in the day, but now? It filled my heart with certainty—this was no hallucination. I didn't know how or for how long, but Nellie was actually speaking to me.

"I always knew your path would lead you back here eventually," Nellie said. She managed to keep the 'I told you so' tone from her voice.

I tilted my head. "We're dragons, not psychics. How did you know?"

With that, Nellie laughed. It was just as I'd remembered it. Light, bubbly. Carefree. Another pang of memory swelled in my heart.

"Rosemary told me, sweetie. She's a smart cookie, but told me I couldn't interfere with fate. Said you'd come back soon enough. Turns out she was right, just not in the way I'd expected." Her expression fell then, sadness crossing her already-lined face. This time she was the one reaching out for something she could never touch.

"Mom," I choked. I reached out my hand as close as I dared. Heat poured off the fireplace and against my skin, but for an instant, I could almost feel her. Then it was gone, swept away like a breeze.

My vision blurred with tears and I swiped them away. I clenched my hands into fists and planted my feet. More than anything, I wanted to run forward and hug her. Touch her. Smell her subtle, calming scent one more time. But she wasn't there. Not really. And even dragons could get burned.

The flames crackled once more and she faded for a moment, my heart shooting into my throat. I lunged forward, unmindful of the heat. And then the image returned, weak and wavery, but there.

"I can't stay much longer, Sebbie. But I wanted to say I

am so proud of you. I love you more than all the stars in the sky."

I sniffled and nodded, trying to smile through the tears.

"And Will." She turned to my mate now. "Thank you, honey. Thank you for taking good care of my son. For helping him see what has been here all along. You two are perfect together."

Will averted his gaze from both of us, blushing.

"There's one more thing," Nellie said in an urgent voice. "It's for the both of you, and I think there will come a day you'll need it. There's a safe under the floorboards in the back storage room that I never told you about. It's under the rug and easy chair. I think you'll find my last little gift to you in there. I certainly don't need it anymore."

Oh wow. I really hadn't expected that. I mean, I should have. This house was filled with more twists and turns than a tangled headphone cable, but a whole secret compartment I'd totally missed?

"I thought I'd found all the secrets," I laughed, shaking my head. "Little me was so proud of that. Snooping around when you were busy with guests."

Nellie beamed. "And this is the biggest secret of them all. Use it well, boys. Take care of each other."

I swallowed the lump in my throat, watching as she faded back into the flames.

"Wait!" I cried. "Mom! I love you. I love you so much."

"I love you too, Sebbie," she called, but it came from a distance like a poorly connected telephone line. Then fireplace whooshed upward in a final explosion of sparks, and then the flames returned to normal, flickering orange-red. No ghosts or spirits in sight.

All was silent. All was still.

MIDNIGHT RUN

WILL

CHRISTMAS EVE

"*H*aven't put up the sign yet, but we're going to be closed tomorrow." The barista grinned at me, handing over a steaming mug of apple cider and a cranberry crepe. "And the annual shifter run is tonight. Will I be seeing you two there?"

I glanced at Seb. He was too occupied looking at the case of baked goods to notice anything else, so I nudged him in the side.

"Hey, what was that for?" He crowed, looking up.

"Evan had a question for you."

Sebastian stood. "Yeah?"

"The shifters run," Evan said again, rubbing the back of his neck. "We do it every Christmas Eve to ring in the holiday."

"Ohhh." Back when I lived in Vale Valley, I'd either been too young or too stubborn to participate. I literally flew the coop to get away from my shifter nature. A lot of good that did. But now I was back, and the longer I stayed here, the more I felt like maybe this could be home after all.

"It would be my first one, but I'd be happy to make an appearance. Why not."

Evan beamed back at us. "It's nothing too formal, we'll meet at the clearing at midnight, shift, and have a little fun. I heard Rosemary's even coming out tonight."

My eyes widened at that. "I thought she didn't shift anymore. Her wolf…"

Evan shrugged. "It's just what I heard. And who knows, Vale Valley is full of all sorts of surprises this year."

My stomach did a flip flop at that. He didn't know the half of it.

Though I was happy for my mate and had always been interested in the midnight run, I'd never been invited. I wasn't a shifter, after all. So perhaps I'd stay home and watch a movie.

Or finally take a damn pregnancy test.

"You wanna come?" Sebastian asked. "Might be fun. We can see what all the fuss is about."

"But I'm not a shifter," I stammered. There went my plans.

"That's okay," Sebastian said. "I am. Mates are welcome, right Evan?"

"Of course," Evan said, eyes gleaming. "Wouldn't want to leave him out of the fun."

I grinned at them both. A strange, curling sensation flowed through my core and outward. Something a little like anticipation? Surprise? Excitement?

Or maybe it was just so new, actually being picked for something. Being invited for something. Wanted.

I could get used to that.

"How will I keep up, though?" I looked up into Seb's honey-brown eyes. "You'll all leave me in the dust."

Sebastian's face lit up with an idea. There was that teasing, secretive grin. "Not if you ride on my back."

"On your..." I mouthed the words. "In dragon form?"

I'd never seen Sebastian shift. Though the town was full of shifters, many kept their animal natures well controlled. Come to think of it, I'd only ever seen a few shifts, period. And never a dragon. My mate, my wonderful, strong alpha...I tried to imagine him towering over me as a powerful dragon, filled with fire. I imagined him soaring above the clouds. And me on his back.

"Would you be okay with that?" Sebastian asked. "I don't want to push you, but the view from up there is spectacular."

I swallowed the knot of apprehension and nodded. "I'd love to. Good thing I'm not scared of heights." I gave a nervous laugh. "Not yet, at least."

Sebastian wrapped me in his arms. It didn't matter that we were in public. I needed the hug right then. His warmth flowed through me and around me as Seb planted a kiss on top of my head. "I guess we'll find out tonight."

"I guess we will," I repeated. I glanced longingly at the cranberry crepe and rapidly-cooling apple cider. "Now can I eat? I'm starving!"

NIGHT FELL QUICKER THAN SEEMED POSSIBLE. THE food hadn't upset my stomach this time, which was always a plus, but there was a different sort of anxious gnawing in my gut as the time drew closer.

Was I really going to go through with this?

I was just...Will. I couldn't shift into an animal. I couldn't fly. And if something happened to me, I was a lot less resilient than the others, too. All evening I had visions of free-falling through the air, landing with a smack in the middle of some field somewhere, losing the baby...

I gulped and a hand went to my stomach. There was that thought again. Was my body trying to tell me something?

I needed to tell him. I knew that. But if he wanted a child...or even if he didn't, and it turned out I was wrong, the false alarm would cause even more stress. I wanted to wait until I knew, but time grew short. It was Christmas Eve, and I still didn't know for sure what Seb's plans for the New Year were...

Taking a deep breath, I walked into one of the back rooms where Seb was tapping away on his laptop. I knocked on the door frame as I entered and he looked up.

"Hey sweetie. Just about ready for tonight?" He glanced at the clock. "We should probably get ready to head out in half an hour or so. You'll want to bundle up—gets cold up there."

"I will. Got my coat and scarf all laid out." I shuffled my feet, searching for what to say next. "There's um, something I wanted to talk to you about."

Sebastian looked up from his computer. "What's up, cinnabun?"

I took a deep breath. Gulped. Here went nothing.

"I think I might be—"

At literally the worst time in the history of times, the phone rang. I flinched at the sound and Seb's eyes snapped to the caller ID. His face fell.

"I am so sorry, sweetheart. If it was anyone else, I'd ignore it but I've gotta take this." His expression was almost pained. What could be so important?

"I—" I started, but he'd already picked up the receiver.

"Sorry," he mouthed again before answering the call.

The hope deflated out of me and the words stuck on my

tongue. Sighing, I turned and left. Guess now wasn't the time, either.

By the time Sebastian got off the phone, we were nearly running late. He tried to mask it, but I could see the haunted expression behind his eyes. Something had happened. Something bad.

How could I bring up my own problems at a time like this?

"You ready?" Seb called. Even his voice sounded tired.

I yearned to go to him then. Wanted to wrap him in my love and make it all go away. He'd been through so much lately, and it seemed like the hits never stopped coming. When it rains, it pours.

"You still wanna go?" I asked tentatively, watching him.

He looked at me like I was crazy. "Yeah, duh. Besides, I think we could both use some fresh air right about now. Come on." He took my shoulder and led me out of the room to the entryway.

Fine. If he didn't want to talk about it, then I wouldn't bring it up. Right now, all I wanted to do was make my mate happy and wash away whatever haunted those beautiful eyes. So I'd stand strong, for him. Our talk could wait.

By the time we arrived at the clearing, most everyone had already gathered. There were plenty of people I knew there, but plenty I didn't, as well. We wove through the crowd, greeting and shaking hands and wishing everyone a joyous season. I put on my best smile and played the part, but nagging doubt still coiled inside me. I had to tell him. I had to. But when?

A sudden round of applause cut off my thoughts, and I looked around to find the source. Rosemary had arrived, wearing a long flowing white gown and a wreath of holly atop her head.

I grinned and started clapping along. I knew how much this meant to her. Ever since her husband passed, she'd stayed home for the midnight run. Said it didn't feel right without him. But so much had changed this year. New traditions were made. Old traditions were rekindled. And just when I least expected it, a man who'd become my mate flew into my life.

Funny how that works, isn't it?

"You look stunning," Sebastian admitted. "Glad you could make it."

She gave us a mischievous smile and shrugged. "Things

are changing here in the Valley. The return of the Festival, new opportunities, new love—" She glanced at us. "Figure its time I try something new as well."

"Thank you for coming," one of the larger shifter men said, stepping forward to shake her hand. "We're about to get started, but perhaps you'd like to lead?"

Rosemary's eyes flashed and a grin spread across her face. "I'd like that very much."

I stood there and watched. Everyone grew silent. The only sounds were the wind whistling through the trees and the far off hoo-hoo call of an owl. Lazy clouds floated past, and the now-exposed moon bathed us all in her light.

What happened next was unlike anything I could have imagined. A chorus of howls and cries ripped through the night. People tossed their clothes aside. Hunkered down. Shifted.

Chaos reigned around me. Sebastian became my anchor in that storm. I clung to him like a lifeline, watching his eyes melt from brown to bright, glowing gold. The same thing that had happened to my neighbors and friends was happening to him too. Soon, he would stand before me as a dragon.

"You ready for this?" He asked me, squeezing my hand.

His voice had taken on a different tenor, deeper than his usual. The dragon was there all right, begging to come out.

"As I'll ever be," I promised him, and Seb gave himself over to the shift.

It was unlike anything I'd seen before. I watched in mixed fascination and terror as his body morphed and changed in front of me. He roared out to the night, so loud it shook the ground where I stood. I didn't move a muscle. Couldn't. I was too enraptured but what I saw.

His feet turned into huge talons and claws. His eyes bulged and glowed even brighter with golden life. And then the most miraculous thing of all happened: from his back sprouted two impossibly large, powerful wings.

The entire shift took only a few seconds, but it was like I was watching in slow motion. I wanted to record every little bit of it. Every tweak. Every change. He was mine. He was strong. So powerful. So beautiful.

A large green dragon stood before me, his scales shimmering proudly in the moonlight. Curled horns protruded from the spot where his forehead had been, and a white stripe raced down his back, all the way to his tail.

I couldn't close my gaping mouth. A real live dragon.

And he was mine.

I stepped forward, almost in a daze. My hand outstretched in front of me, I took a careful step. Then another. My shaking hand came to rest against his warm, smooth scales, and I sucked in a breath. The scales were smooth like glass under my fingertips, but warm and pulsing with life. I could feel each beat of his heart. Each rise and fall of his breath.

I laid my head against his side and closed my eyes, listening to the thrum of his heart with mine. It sung to me in words that needed no explanation. It was our song, our duet. The very same melody that could never be reproduced by another, combined by the music of our souls.

<Are you okay, little one?>

My eyes snapped open. I'd heard him, just then. But dragons couldn't talk, at least not like us...

I'd heard him in my mind.

"Whoa," I breathed, taking a step back. "I can hear you?"

<You can hear me, my love. Try it for yourself.>

I squinted. *<How's this?>*

<Perfect. Would you like to climb on?>

All the earlier fear I had felt melted out of me. I trusted him. Dragon or human, he was my mate. He would never hurt me.

<I'm not sure...where to...>

Sebastian bent at the knees, his back crouching lower to the ground. *<Clamber on and get seated. Right over the wings is a good spot.>*

I tested a foothold on Seb's side, trying to see if it would hold my weight.

<Don't be shy, cinnabun. You won't hurt me.>

With that thought in mind I grabbed onto a few of the scales and hoisted myself up, my feet kicking at his side. It wasn't pretty, but I managed to scramble up onto his back. Up here, the sensations of life and power were even stronger. I felt it too, a rising within my own spirit. We were one.

I scooted forward to the spot where Seb had suggested, nuzzling my face into the warmth of the scales at his neck. God, when did he start smelling so good? It spoke to me in the most primal way, his pheromones mixing with mine for a heady cocktail of awe and desire. I wrapped my hands around him and braced my knees on either side.

<You ready?> Seb echoed inside my mind.

<I'm ready.> I echoed back.

<Hold on tight!>

Those huge, beautiful wings expanded to their full span and flapped, pushing the air under us as we sailed upward. He kicked off with his back legs and the ground fell away, wind rushing through my hair and roaring in my ears.

I was flying. Holy shit. *We* were flying!

The ground grew smaller around us as Seb ascended, rushing past in a blur of moonlit ivory.

Each footprint in the snow diminished to a tiny speck. Cold air flooded against my face and whipped my scarf out behind me, but I didn't care. Sebastian's warmth was more than enough, and I wouldn't have traded this experience for the world.

I saw now what he meant about the view from up here. When you were so high above the town, you felt so small, and yet so big at the same time. All the fears and problems that plagued me on the ground couldn't touch me up here. Here, I was simply present. Enjoying the warmth of my mate, feeling the pulse of life between us, and watching as the moon smiled down upon us all.

<What do you think?> I heard Seb's voice over the roar of the wind. *<Beautiful, isn't it?>*

I didn't know that I could come up with words for how stunned I was. *<It's incredible...I've never seen anything like it.>*

<Now you know why shifters love to run. Or fly, as the case may be.>

We sailed onto a passing air current and glided, Seb's wide wingspan keeping us aloft. Mountains loomed in the distance and below us thick forests of pine trees stretched toward the sky. Shifters of all types ran and jumped and played around us. The night lit up with their cries of joy and celebration.

<Merry Christmas, darling.> Seb said as we circled Vale Valley's huge lake. Even in the depths of the coldest winter, it never froze. Our silhouettes reflected off the glassy surface, along with the pale shape of the full moon. *<I'm glad you're here with me.>*

<I love you.> I whispered to him in my mind, laying my head against the warmth of his scales once more.

<I love you too. Now and forever.>

CHRISTMAS MORNING SURPRISE

SEBASTIAN

*E*ven though we'd been out until nearly dawn the night before, I woke early on Christmas Day.

Something was different.

I sniffed the air, rolled over.

It was my mate.

Will was still sleeping on his side, curled up into a little ball with a pillow hugged to his chest. He looked so peaceful like that, so happy. I hated to rouse him.

But there was definitely something off about him. About that smell. I sniffed the air again.

Had his scent changed, somehow?

No, that wasn't right.

"What are you doing?" Will mumbled sleepily.

I jerked away. Hadn't realized he was awake. But now that he was...

"Are you...are you feeling all right?" I asked, not sure how to phrase my question. "You smell funny."

Will rolled over, a confused look on his face. "Maybe you're still smelling all the woodsy smells from last night. We rolled around in the grass for a while after, remember?"

Oh, did I ever.

"No, this is different. It's...I dunno. Probably nothing. You're right."

Probably something, my dragon crooned within me.

As my mind cleared, I remembered Will's awkward demeanor before the run last night. I remembered him wanting to tell me something, before I'd gotten that damned phone call.

Did that have something to do with all of this?

"That was fun," Will mumbled, rolling back over to bury his face in the pillow. God, he was so adorable when he was sleepy.

I traced the curve of his shoulder down to his back with my eyes, taking in each slope and angle. No matter what little imperfections he thought he had, he would always be perfect to me.

"Can we do it again sometime?" Will asked after a moment. It came out kinda muffled, but I got the idea.

"Oh," I said, backtracking. I blinked a few times, trying to get my mind back on the conversation. "Flying, you mean? You weren't scared?"

Will shrugged. "A little. But," he shook his head, "No. Not really. I knew you wouldn't let me fall."

I rolled over and curled up against him, kissing the back of his neck. "Never."

That might have been a mistake. This close to him, the smell was even stronger. It wasn't bad, no. Just...different. And something about it pulled at my core instincts to protect and love and nurture...

Wait a second.

"Will," I started talking before I could rationalize my way out of it again.

"Mmhm?"

"What was it you wanted to talk to me about last night?

Seemed important, and then I had that phone call, and then we got caught up in the run..." I shook my head. "I'm sorry. I should have listened to you. But I'm here now. What's up?"

A gnawing, growing certainty told me I already knew what it was, but I wanted to hear him say it. Wanted to prove this wasn't just a wishful fantasy.

Will turned over to face me. His brilliant green eyes captured mine and I laid there, enthralled. The room was so quiet I could hear the racing beat of his heart.

He pursed his lips for a moment, thinking. Then he gently took my hand and placed it over his stomach. "I don't know how to tell you this," Will started, his voice barely more than a whisper. "But I think I might be pregnant."

In that moment, my entire world shifted.

Pregnant. I repeated the word in my mind.

It sounded almost too good to be true. I splayed my fingers over Will's belly, caressing the soft, warm skin there. Then I bent down and gave him a kiss, right over the belly button.

This time the scent hit me full on. Yep. It was definitely coming from my mate, and definitely emanating out from around his midsection. Right where his womb would be.

All the pieces clicked into place and I stared up at him, eyes watering. Could I really be so blessed?

That lingering scent, the one that burrowed into my heart and soul, was not just coming from Will. I realized that now. It was coming from both of them—my mate, and the small spark of life growing inside him.

I choked out a disbelieving laugh, bringing him close in a bear hug. Will squeaked and squirmed against me.

"What?" He laughed, nuzzling into my neck. "What's the matter?"

I drew back then, to make sure I looked him in the eyes when I said it. "You're right. That's what I was smelling. And this is the best Christmas gift I could have ever asked for." I closed the gap and claimed his lips. I needed to let him know just how much this meant to me.

Will let out a breathy moan and opened up, our tongues tangling as now not only two, but three spirals of energy built and combined.

A child. A family.

"You really mean it?" Will said, his eyes wet.

"Mmhm," I nodded, kissing his forehead, his eyelids, his nose. "We're going to have a baby!"

My mate's beautiful grin stretched wider till I thought it might split his face in half. His eyes crinkled at the corners. His shoulders shook. Then he laughed. With joy and relief and love.

I held him there, laughing and crying and taking in the moment. I never thought I could want something so much. Never dared to.

But Will made me want things I'd never even dreamed.

The image of a cute little child formed in my mind. Big, green eyes like his daddy. A mop of curly hair. Small fingers and toes that reached out for everything with unquenchable curiosity. And a smile so big it could light the darkest night.

"It's a Christmas miracle," Will breathed, but even he rolled his eyes at how cheesy that sounded. "It really is, though. I thought I might be, and I was afraid of what you'd say, and—"

"Stop." I held up my hand. "You didn't tell me sooner because you were afraid I wouldn't approve?"

Will looked away, sheepish. "Well...yeah. I didn't know what your plans were."

I huffed out a breath and drew him close to my body again, my lips trailing up and down the curve of his ear. Will shivered in my arms, then relaxed.

"You think I'm just going to leave you? After news like this?" I whispered each word, punctuating them with butterfly kisses.

"I..." Will stammered. "I was scared. I didn't know. You've got your firm in New York, your apartment, your..."

"Hey," I stopped him again. "That can all be adjusted. I'd already made up my mind, was going to go sign the papers with Rosemary today, but this? This just seals the deal."

"So you're staying? Really? You're keeping the Dozing Dragon?" Will's voice came out soft, hopeful. And it was that spark of hope that had drawn me to him ever since the beginning.

"I'll have to make some changes," I admitted. "And it won't be easy. But yes, Will. I'm staying. For you, and for Rose, and for the Dozing Dragon, and for our child. I'm staying."

"And for you?" Will followed up without missing a beat. "What do you want?"

I already knew the answer to that one. "Everything I want is right here." I held him against me, relishing the slow, steady beat of his heart, until we both drifted back to sleep.

"CAN WE FINALLY GO DOWN THERE?" WILL ASKED me after waking up the second time. "We waited until Christmas morning. Now I'm dying to see what Nellie left us."

"You don't want to finish your tea first?" I asked, peering over the rim of my mug.

"I can bring it with," Will offered. "I just can't stop thinking about it."

I stood and placed my mug back in the sink. "Fine, Mr. Impatient. Let's go." Once he set his mind to something, I'd never get a word in edgewise. Better just to go along with it.

And I was curious, too. With all the mystery and magic surrounding this place, who knew what could be down there?

We walked through the twisting hallways to end up at the spare storage room at the back of the house. The room had never really been used for much, but there was an old musty rug and a leather armchair positioned in the middle of the creaky floorboards. A painting from a local artist hung on the wall and covering every other square inch of floor space were boxes, boxes, and more boxes. Will's eyes widened when I opened the door and we saw the mess.

Mine did too. I just hid it better.

"So it's true what they say about dragons and their hoards," Will teased, squeezing a path between the debris with his small frame.

"Hey, not all dragons are hoarders," I pointed out and tried to follow him. But I was a good bit larger, and had to shift some of the boxes to make a path.

Will huffed out a laugh at that. "Oh, and you're not? Dude, have you *seen* the amount of paperwork you brought with you? We have computers for a reason, but you keep printing everything out. The stack of books and papers in your office alone is probably as tall as you are. Save the trees, man!"

"I just like to read and make notes in hard copy!" I protested, but I knew it wouldn't get me far. He'd caught me there.

Will made it to the center of the room and peered at the ancient rug. "She said it was under here?"

"Yeah, think so. Gonna have to move the chair first, though."

"I got it." He leaned into the chair and pushed. It didn't move. His face strained, his muscles bulged. Nothing. "I don't got it," he panted, drooping.

Will crouched down and inspected the chair's legs while I moved closer. "Is this thing bolted to the floor or something? I don't see any screws..."

"It's a heavy chair, and the friction of the rug is making it even harder," I explained. I joined him on the other side, getting a firm grip. "You push, I'll pull. Ready?"

He straightened and braced himself against the frame again. "Ready."

With more than a few grunts and a high-pitched squeal of wood and metal, we got the chair moved off the rug and into a cleared-out space I'd created. I wiped my brow and turned around to dig my fingers under the old rug. "Now for the main event."

I peeled back the heavy rug and dust flew everywhere. I sneezed, which just kicked up more particles. But dust and grime aside, I forgot it almost entirely when I saw the trapdoor hidden there.

"Whoa." Will came closer. "This house is so cool. Who has a secret trapdoor room?"

"My mom did, apparently. Now stand back, I'm gonna open it."

Will scooted into an empty corner and I gripped the metal handle, feeling a spark of magical energy the moment we touched. Not just a secret trapdoor. An enchanted secret trapdoor. Just what was she hiding down here?

I groaned and lifted upward, the old door coming free from decades worth of dirt and disrepair at last. It creaked open and I lost my grip, sending it banging over onto the adjacent pile of boxes with a crash.

"Sorry," I whispered, wincing. "Hopefully nothing breakable in there."

"Look!" Will pointed.

I followed his lead. The trapdoor opened up into an old crawl space. I couldn't see much from this vantage point but there was some sort of light coming from inside. Seemed pretty far away, judging from the dimness, but it was impossible to tell from up here. Just how far across the house did this tunnel go?

"Alphas first." Will nudged me. "I'm not goin' in there alone."

"Suit yourself," I said, and hopped down into the crawl space.

I flicked on the flashlight app on my phone as soon as I got down there, and once my eyes had adjusted to the light, I couldn't believe what I saw.

"Will!" I cried hoarsely. "Get down here!"

"Coming!" I heard him say from above. A scuffling sound. Then footsteps. "What is the big. deal?" He came up beside me and he too, stopped short.

"Whoa."

Now *this* was a dragon's hoard. A pile of golden trinkets, goblets, and gems lay before us, like some kind of pirates plunder. I blinked a few times. Rubbed my eyes. Where did she get all this stuff?

"Are you seeing...what I'm seeing?" Will said, his voice shaking.

"Talk about a dragon hoard," I muttered in awe. I stepped forward when I noticed a dusty sign sticking out of the ground. I kneeled and directed the light, brushing the dust away so that I could read it.

Will and I read the sign aloud.

> *"Dear Sebastian, before you were born—I was a bit of a wild child. I traveled the globe in search of rare and precious treasures, and brought them back here. It was a heady lifestyle, always zipping from one place to the next, full of adventure, but then one day I found out I was pregnant from one of the assistants on my last expedition, and I hung up my adventuring gear for good. I never was able to get in touch with him again, but I made a pact: I would be the best mother to you that I could, no matter what. Even if you found me a bit odd or irritating at times, I want you to know I love you more than words can say. I hope that this gift will serve the next generation of the Valley just as much as it has served me. Love, your mother."*

I read it again, the words blurring as tears welled up in my eyes. She'd often allude to her "younger days", but I had no idea she meant anything like this...

"So she's basically the best hoarder of all time," Will joked, still staring in awe at the gems.

"Something like that." I shook my head, smiled, and laughed. "I think I figured out how we're gonna both save my company and The Dozing Dragon."

"Just like that?" Will asked, taking my hand.

"Nellie's secret stash *and* a baby on the way? This is seriously the best Christmas ever."

BABY MAKES THREE

SEBASTIAN

9 MONTHS LATER

"Fuck, alpha! Give it to me!" Will moaned and shook under my thrusts, each one a little deeper than the one before.

He was very pregnant by now, and I'd be lying if I said I didn't think it was hot.

I admit, I didn't think the baby life was gonna be for me, but after going through nine months of pregnancy prep with my mate? I couldn't wait.

God help me, I was already wondering when we could do it again.

I brushed a loving hand over the swell of Will's stomach,

my cock lengthening and inflating inside Will's tight channel. We created this. This life. This baby. And what a miracle that was.

Will's nails dug into me, clearly more carnal thoughts on his mind. His eyes rolled up toward the ceiling and his cock was red and leaking. I was so close, so close...

"Right there! Yeah! Fuck!" Will gasped, and I couldn't hold on any longer. I slammed inside him one last time and held him there, spilling my seed while the knot of my cock sealed around us. Will wailed and thrashed, the pressure of the knot sending him over the edge as well. His hips bucked forward and off the bed as hot, sticky cum sprayed between us.

My mate. My omega. And soon...my child.

"Fuuuuck..." Will drawled out, and each contraction of his channel milked a little more cum out of me.

Only thing was...it kept going.

And going.

"I..." Will panted, craning his neck around to look at me with wide eyes. "I can't stop...cumming..."

That's when a rush of wetness enveloped my cock with such force that it pushed me out, knot and all.

Cum and fluid pooled on the bed, leaving both of us dazed for a moment. Until I realized what that was, and what was happening.

"Oh god," I breathed. "Will, I think you're..."

"No fucking shit!" Will groaned, clasping his stomach. "You motherfucking asshole, you fucked the baby into coming!"

"I..." I wrung my hands, trying to think of a response. We'd been expecting this, and it was about that time, but wow, this timing...

I winced and stumbled across the room, throwing on some pants.

"It's gonna be okay. Keep calm!" I repeated it to myself just as much as to him. "Let's get you into some clothes and over to the hospital. I'll call them right now, let them know we're coming."

"You fucking...fuck!"

Will continued to unleash a string of curses on me the entire time I was on the phone. And the entire ride to the hospital. For such a sweet omega, he had a filthy mouth!

But still, I didn't say a word. Didn't try to stop him. I guess I kind of deserved it.

And I had just a little bit of sick alpha pride that I'd fucked him so hard that I'd sent him into labor. Just a little.

"We've got a room prepared for you already." A nurse came out to meet us as soon as we arrived at the hospital. She and another nurse helped Will onto a gurney and wheeled him down the hall, motioning for me to follow.

I kept up behind them at a jog, every instinct in my soul flashing off at high alert. *My mate was in labor! My mate was having a baby! Oh god, we were going to be parents!*

My dragon was even more impatient than I was. Had to make a real effort to keep from shifting right there in the hospital. But I swallowed my fear, focused on the little one soon to come, and resolved to do whatever I could to be the best dad possible.

Just like Nellie had when she gave up her career for me.

TIME SEEMED TO PASS IN A BLUR. ONE MOMENT, I was wrapped around my omega in the throes of lust. The next, I was sitting in one of those horribly uncomfortable hospital chairs, wringing my hands and hoping for the best.

Will was in there making a hell of a racket. He screamed so much I didn't even know his vocal cords could make those sounds. And of course, there was the cursing. So. Much. Cursing.

I'd wanted to be by his side in the delivery room. Wanted to let him squeeze my bones into dust as he pushed our new baby into the world.

But um...I might have kind of fainted. There was screaming, and blood, and suddenly the world was growing dark around me and...

A shuddering, shrieking cry brought me back, my eyes flying open as I tried to reorient myself.

"God, he's passed out!"

"Someone get the baby!"

"I need a fluid IV!"

Muffled voices and footsteps whirled around me, but it was that single, gasping cry that anchored me to the present. I blinked and images slowly came back into focus. I picked myself up from where I'd slumped over the chair, turned my head to find the source, and....

There he was.

Shrieking and squalling to high heaven, was a tiny, messy, flailing newborn.

Our newborn.

Life rushed back into me as I centered on the squealing thing. I watched as a nurse cut the cord and cleaned him off. I watched as she wrapped him in a blue swaddling blanket. I watched as she handed him, still crying bloody murder, into Will's waiting arms.

Will.

I whirled around so fast I almost fainted again. My head swum and I gripped the arms of the hospital chair for dear life. Our eyes met, and he gave me the most tired, most satisfied smile I'd ever seen.

"We did it," Will breathed, holding the baby against his chest. "We did it."

His eyes were glassy with exhaustion and shock and love, so much love.

"Are you okay? I heard them saying you passed out or something."

I cleared my throat and sat up straighter. "Uh, no. I'm fine. Just worrying about you."

"I'm okay," Will sighed in a dreamy voice. "We're okay. Look, Seb. He has your eyes."

The baby's small head turned toward me, and for the first time, I looked into the face of my son.

There it was again. That earth-shaking movement within me. My whole heart and soul cried out when I saw him, imprinting every feature of his impossibly lovely face on my memory for the rest of time. Nothing would ever be the same. And when this little guy was part of our life? I didn't want it to be.

"Hey," I breathed, looking into those huge chocolate-colored eyes. Will was right. They looked just like mine. Like looking at a little version of myself, mixed together with the one man I loved most in the world. "Hey there, little guy. It's your papa."

"Say hello," Will cooed. "Hello, papa!"

My son simply started wailing again, instead.

Will looked over the shrieking baby's head to catch my gaze. "We'd narrowed it down to two names, but never decided on one, did we?"

I thought for a moment. Now that he mentioned it, he was right. I'd been so busy with guests and contractors, not to mention preparing our home for the birth, that I had never actually settled on one. "It was Rayne versus Storm, right?"

Will nodded. "You and those weather names."

"What?" I retorted. "I like them."

"I do too," Will said. The baby finally began to quiet, laying his little head against Will's bare chest. "Just saying."

"So Rayne versus Storm, huh?" I thought about it for a moment. I looked into my little man's wide eyes. His small, stubby fingers. His little wisps of hair. "He's our little Rayne," I said at last, and as soon as the name left my lips, I knew it was perfect.

"Rayne," Will repeated, planting a kiss on our son's head. "Little Rayne. I love it."

I reached over and took Will's hand. "I love you."

"I love you too," Will started, "but I'm still not going to forgive you for the 'circumstances' around my labor." He snickered out a tired laugh, and I couldn't help it. I laughed too.

"Fair enough," I said and threw my hands up in surrender. "I'll just have to be more careful next time."

Will's eyes widened. "You're already planning a next time?"

I shrugged. "Maybe. But I'm going to make sure I enjoy every little bit of this life first." I leaned forward, braced my arms on the side of the bed, and kissed my mate.

VALE VALLEY

You don't have to leave Vale Valley yet!

We have a whole lineup of stories from some of your favorite authors. They're sweet, spicy, and everything in between. Collect them all!

#1: Mated Under The Mistletoe by Connor Crowe

#2 : Twice as Joyful by Lorelei M Hart

#3 : Three Roses by Alice Shaw

#4 : A Swan For Christmas by M.M. Wilde

#5 : Five Gold Rings by Xander Collins

#6 : His Christmas Lullaby by Leyla Hunt

#7 : A Holiday Magic Mixup by Quinn Michaels

#8; Breakable Faith by Michael Mandrake

#9 : Omega, It's Cold Outside by Coyote Starr

#10 : O Little Town of Vale Valley by Summer Chase

#11 : The Drummer's Heartbeat by Giovanna Reaves

AUTHOR'S NOTE

Thank you so much for picking up this book! I hope you've come to enjoy the world and the characters of Vale Valley just as much as I have.

If you have a moment, consider leaving a review on Amazon. It helps more people find books they love.

Don't ever let anyone dull your shine. Be your best sparkly self!

— Connor Crowe

One last summer. One last chance.

Sign up here for a FREE Love in Diamond Falls prequel - *Summer Heat*

https://dl.bookfunnel.com/ntkicsmnr6

Join my Facebook group Connor's Coven for live streams, giveaways, and sneak peeks. It's the most fun you can have without being arrested ;)

https://www.facebook.com/groups/connorscoven/

24057436R00124